作者序

　　最近幾年，我有機會在社區大學及大學的進修部任教英語，接觸到許多年齡較長的英語初學者，也由於我的課程是以旅遊為主題，因此，我一直在尋找一本教科書，讓即使是不擅長英語的初學者，也可以輕鬆地學習與旅行相關的英語。但是，就我自己的觀查，目前市售的旅遊英語教材，有些資訊量繁雜，還有些字體過小，或是以全英文書寫不適合初學者，因此在課堂上很難使用。有鑑於此，有了出版合適旅遊英語教材的構想，在和出版社討論之後，才有本書的出版。

　　如上所述，這本書是為初學者、不太擅長英語的學生，以及想輕鬆學習旅行英語的人而寫的。本書很容易閱讀，字體適中，結構單純，並且文本、單詞、語法說明等顯而易懂。而且由於它有許多中文翻譯，您可以輕鬆地自己查找單詞含義，不僅可以學習單詞和短句，還可以訓練會話和聽力理解。

　　語言是與人交流的工具之一。我希望許多人能使用本書來學習實際旅行所需的會話技巧。最後，我要感謝瑞蘭出版社的所有編輯在忙於出版本書期間給予的建議和支持。

本間岐理

《誰都學得會的旅遊英語》全書共 13 課，是為英語初學者設計的旅遊英語教材。希望透過輕鬆愉快的旅遊主題，讓初學者享受到開口說英語的樂趣。每課的課程設計如下：

STEP 1 ▶▶▶

「掃描音檔 QR Code」：在開始使用這本教材之前，別忘了先找到書封右下角的 QR Code，拿出手機掃描，就能立即下載書中所有音檔喔！（請自行使用智慧型手機，下載喜歡的 QR Code 掃描器，更能有效偵測書中 QR Code！）

STEP 2 ▶▶▶

「會話」及「中文翻譯」：每課都有 1～2 篇情境旅遊會話，並隨附中文翻譯。

STEP 3 ▶▶▶

「生詞」：為會話中的重點生詞標註詞性及中文意思，再配上所屬意思的圖片，快速開啟圖像記憶。

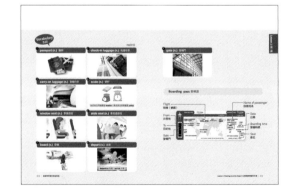

✈ Travel English for Everyone

誰都學得會的
旅遊
英語

本間岐理 著

STEP 4 ▶▶▶

「實用短句」：依照該課主題，延伸出
適合不同旅遊情境的短句。

STEP 5 ▶▶▶

「文法」：挑出會話中的重點句型，拆
解其結構並提供延伸舉例。

STEP 6 ▶▶▶

「練習」及「解答」：每課最後都有填
空、問答、聽寫練習，並隨附解答及中
文翻譯，是最紮實的反覆聽讀訓練。

目錄

mp3-01

Dialogue A: Where Are You Flying to Today?
(A: Ground staff / B: Passenger)

A Hello. Where are you flying to today?

B I'm flying to Australia.

A May I see your passport and ticket, please?

B Here you are.

A All right. Do you have any check-in luggage?

B Yes, I just have one suitcase.

A Please put it on the scale. Are there any batteries or electronic devices inside?

B No.

A Would you prefer a window seat or an aisle seat?

B Window seat, please.

A Okay. Here is your boarding pass. Your flight departs at 3pm from gate 8B, and the boarding starts at 1:45pm. Have a nice trip!

B Thank you!

Chinese Translation
中文翻譯

會話A：您今天飛往哪裡？
（A：地勤人員 / B：旅客）

A：您好。您今天要飛往哪裡？

B：我要飛往澳大利亞。

A：請問我可以看看您的護照和機票嗎？

B：這個給你。

A：好的。您有托運行李嗎？

B：是的，我只有一個行李箱。

A：請把它放在磅秤上。裡面有電池或電子設備嗎？

B：沒有。

A：您想要靠窗的座位還是靠走道的座位？

B：請給我靠窗的座位。

A：好的。這是您的登機證。您的航班在下午 3 點從 8B 登機口起飛，登機時間為下午 1:45。祝您旅途愉快！

B：謝謝！

❶ passport (n.) 護照

❷ check-in luggage (n.) 托運行李

❸ carry-on luggage (n.) 登機行李

❹ scale (n.) 磅秤

英式英文用複數型 **scales**、美式英文用單數型 **scale**

❺ window seat (n.) 靠窗座位

❻ aisle seat (n.) 靠走道座位

❼ board (v.) 登機

❽ depart (v.) 出發

departure 出境、**arrival** 入境

⑨ gate (n.) 登機門

Boarding pass 登機證

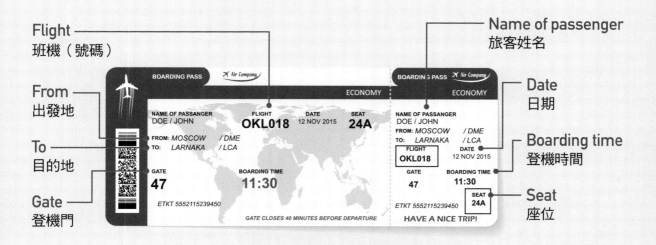

Flight
班機（號碼）

From
出發地

To
目的地

Gate
登機門

Name of passenger
旅客姓名

Date
日期

Boarding time
登機時間

Seat
座位

Departure information board 出境班機資訊版

Departures
出境

Flight
班機號碼

Time
時間

Terminal
航廈

Status
（班機）狀態

Destinations
目的地

FLIGHT	TIME	DESTINATION	TERMINAL	STATUS
A12	4:42	NEW YORK	K1	ON TIME
B01	12:05	BARCELONA	S2	DELAYED
G34	15:30	MILAN	T3	BOARDING
D67	22:00	SEOUL	Z4	
R92	06:29	TOKYO	I5	DELAYED
J34	16:40	SINGAPORE	L6	ON TIME

Remarks 班機狀態

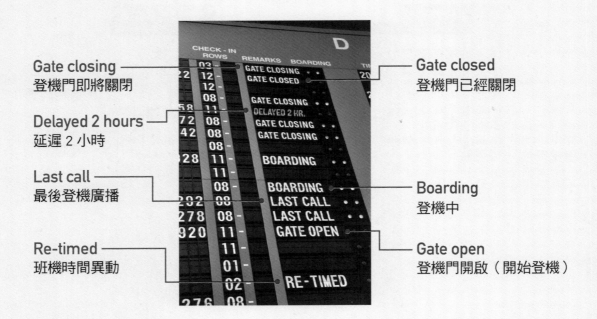

Gate closing
登機門即將關閉

Delayed 2 hours
延遲 2 小時

Last call
最後登機廣播

Re-timed
班機時間異動

Gate closed
登機門已經關閉

Boarding
登機中

Gate open
登機門開啟（開始登機）

1 當你被問到是否有護照及機票，並要遞出時，可以說：

1 **Here you are.** 這個給你。

2 **Here you go.** 這個給你。

3 **Sure.** 當然，有的。

2 想選位時，你可以說：

1 **Could I get an aisle seat?** 我能選靠走道的位子嗎？

2 **Could we get seats together?** 我們的位子能選在一起嗎？

3 托運行李時常見的短句：

1 **How many bags are you checking?** 請問您有幾件行李要託運？

2 **Your baggage is overweight.** 您的行李過重。

3 **It weighs about 30kg.** 大概 30 公斤重。

4 **This suitcase is 5kg overweight.** 這個行李箱超重 5 公斤。

5 **Could I take a few things out?** 我能拿一些東西出來嗎？

6 **Is there any excess baggage charge?** 超重要多收錢嗎？

4 對出境旅客說的話：

1 **Have a nice trip.** 祝您旅途愉快。

Grammar
文法

01 **May I ...?** （詢問許可）可以……嗎？

例 May I borrow a pen? 能借我一支筆嗎？

May I have the bill, please? 可以給我帳單嗎？

02 **Do you have ...?** 你有……嗎？

例 Do you have your passport? 你有帶護照嗎？

Do you have room service? 請問有客房服務嗎？

03 **Are there any ...?** 有……嗎？

例 Are there any phones in the lobby? 大廳裡有電話嗎？

Are there any toilets in this building? 這棟樓有廁所嗎？

04 **Would you prefer A or B?** 你想要 A 還是 B？（較有禮貌）

例 Would you prefer coffee or tea? 你想要咖啡還是茶？

Would you prefer meat or fish? 你想要肉還是魚？

05 **Here is (are) ...** （把東西遞給他人時）這是……

例 Here is your change. 這是你的找零。

Here is something for you. 這是要給你的東西。

06 inside vs. outside

需要明確區分內外關係時，會使用 inside（裡面）與 outside（外面）。

例　My passport is inside the suitcase.　　　我的護照放在行李箱裡面。

You cannot smoke inside an airplane.　　　你不可以在飛機內吸菸。

07 at　用來表達時間

例　I will get up at 9.　　　我會在 9 點起來。

I have lunch at noon.　　　我在中午時吃午餐。

Exercise
練習

一、生詞填空：請將適當的生詞填入空格中。

> board / gate / window seat / scale / check-in luggage
> aisle / depart / passport / suitcases

1. I lost my _____ .

2. One person can bring only 2 pieces of _____ .

3. I would like to check these two _____ .

4. There is a _____ in the kitchen.

5. Do you prefer window seat or _____ seat?

6. I prefer a _____ because I love looking at the scenery.

7. I will _____ a flight to Japan.

8. Get ready. We are about to _____ .

9. All passengers for flight NH356 please proceed to _____ 16.

二、問答：請用英語回答下列問題。

1. 想跟朋友家人一起坐的時候，該怎麼說？

_____

2. 要怎麼向地勤問有沒有加收超重費用？

_____

3. 如何表達想從行李中拿出一些東西？

_____

4. 要怎麼向地勤問有沒有行李過重？

_____

三、文法填空：請將適當的句型填入空格中。

> Are there any / at / inside / Would you prefer / Where / May I see
> Have a nice trip / Here is / Do you have

A: Hello. ① _____ are you flying to today?

B: I'm flying to Australia.

A: ② _____ your passport, please?

B: Here you are.

A: All right. ③ _____ any check-in luggage?

B: Yes, I have one piece.

A: Please put it on the scale. ④ _____ batteries or electronic devices ⑤ _____ ?

B: No.

A: ⑥ _____ a window seat or an aisle seat?

B: Window seat, please.

A: Okay. ⑦ _____ your boarding pass. Your flight departs ⑧ _____ 3pm from gate 8B, and the boarding starts ⑨ _____ 1:45pm.

⑩ _____ !

B: Thank you!

四、聽寫：請聽音檔，並將答案填入空格中。

A: Hello, sir. Where are you flying to today?

B: ① _____

A: May I see your passport, please?

B: ② _____

A: Alright. Do you have any check-in luggage?

B: ③ _____

A: Please put it on the scale. Are there any batteries or electronic devices inside?

B: ④ _____

A: Would you prefer a window seat or an aisle seat?

B: ⑤ _____

A: Okay. Here is your boarding pass. Your flight departs at 3pm from gate 8B, and the boarding starts at 1:45pm. Have a nice trip!

B: ⑥ _____

第一課 練習解答・中文翻譯

一、生詞填空：請將適當的生詞填入空格中。

1. I lost my **passport**.
   我遺失了我的護照。

2. One person can bring only 2 pieces of **check-in luggage**.
   一個人只能帶兩件托運行李。

3. I would like to check these two **suitcases**.
   我想要托運這兩個行李箱。

4. There is a **scale** in the kitchen.
   廚房裡有個秤子。

5. Do you prefer window seat or **aisle** seat?
   您想要靠窗的座位，還是靠走道的座位？

6. I prefer a **window seat** because I love looking at the scenery.
   我想要靠窗的座位，因為我喜歡看風景。

7. I will **board** a flight to Japan.
   我將搭機飛往日本。

8. Get ready. We are about to **depart**.
   （請）準備好，我們準備要出發了。

9. All passengers for flight NH356 please proceed to **gate** 16.
   請所有搭乘 NH356 航班的旅客，前往 16 號登機門。

二、問答：請用英語回答下列問題。

1. **Could we get seats together?** 　　　　我們的位子能選在一起嗎？

2. **Is there any excess baggage charge?** 　　超重要多收錢嗎？

3. **Could I take a few things out?** 　　　　我能拿一些東西出來嗎？

4. **Is my baggage overweight?** 　　　　　我的行李過重嗎？

三、文法填空：請將適當的句型填入空格中。

A: Hello. ① **Where** are you flying to today?

B: I'm flying to Australia.

A: ② **May I see** your passport, please?

B: Here you are.

A: All right. ③ **Do you have** any check-in luggage?

B: Yes, I have one piece.

A: Please put it on the scale. ④ **Are there any** batteries or electronic devices ⑤ **inside**?

B: No.

A: ⑥ **Would you prefer** a window seat or an aisle seat?

B: Window seat, please.

A: Okay. ⑦ **Here is** your boarding pass. Your flight departs ⑧ **at** 3pm from gate 8B, and the boarding starts ⑨ **at** 1:45pm. ⑩ **Have a nice trip**!

B: Thank you!

中文翻譯請見 **P. 11**。

四、聽寫：請聽音檔，並將答案填入空格中。

A: Hello, sir. Where are you flying to today?

B: ① **I'm flying to Australia.**

A: May I see your passport, please?

B: ② **Here you are.**

A: Alright. Do you have any check-in luggage?

B: ③ **Yes, I have one piece.**

A: Please put it on the scale. Are there any batteries or electronic devices inside?

B: ④ **No.**

A: Would you prefer a window seat or an aisle seat?

B: ⑤ **Window seat, please.**

A: Okay. Here is your boarding pass. Your flight departs at 3pm from gate 8B, and the boarding starts at 1:45pm. Have a nice trip!

B: ⑥ **Thank you.**

中文翻譯請見 P. 11。

Eating on Board
在飛機上用餐

mp3-04

Dialogue 會話

Dialogue A: Food and Beverage Service
(A: Flight attendant / B: Passenger)

A Dear passengers, in-flight meal service will begin shortly. Please return to your seats and put your seatbacks in the upright position. Thank you.

A We have chicken noodles and fish with rice. Which one would you like to eat?

B Fish, please.

A Here you are. Would you like something to drink?

B What kind of drinks do you have?

A We have juice, cola, beer, wine, and water.

B Wine, please.

A White or red?

B Red, please.

A Would you like some coffee or tea?

B Coffee, please.

A Would you like some creamer and sugar?

B No, thank you.

A Are you finished with the meal?

B Yes, here's my tray.

Chinese Translation
中文翻譯

會話A：餐飲服務
（A：空服員 / B：旅客）

A：親愛的旅客您好，機上的供餐服務即將開始。請回到您的座位，並把椅背豎直。謝謝。

A：我們有雞肉麵跟魚肉飯，您想要吃哪個？
B：請給我魚肉（飯）。
A：這個給您。請問您還需要喝點什麼嗎？
B：有什麼種類的飲料？
A：我們有果汁、可樂、啤酒、葡萄酒，還有水。
B：請給我葡萄酒。
A：要白酒還是紅酒呢？
B：請給我紅酒。

A：需要來點咖啡或茶嗎？

B：請給我咖啡。
A：需要奶精和糖嗎？
B：不用，謝謝。

A：您吃完了嗎？
B：是的，托盤給你。

Vocabulary 生詞

❶ service (n.) 服務

❷ finish (v.) 完成

過去式和過去分詞為**finished**

❸ tray (n.) 托盤

❹ in-flight meal (n.) 機內餐

❺ chicken (n.) 雞肉

❻ pork (n.) 豬肉

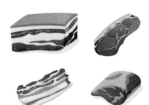

❼ beef (n.) 牛肉

❽ fish (n.) 魚

9 noodles (n.) 麵

10 rice (n.) 飯

11 bread (n.) 麵包

12 beverage (n.) 飲料 (= drink)

IT'S TIME TO *Drink*

13 juice (n.) 果汁

14 cola (n.) 可樂

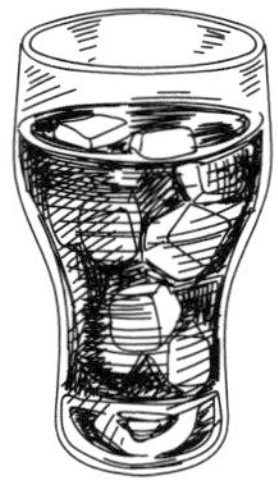

15 beer (n.) 啤酒

16 wine (n.) 葡萄酒

white (adj.) 白色 、 red (adj.) 紅色

17 ice (n.) 冰

18 water (n.) 水

19 soda (n.) 汽水

20 coffee (n.) 咖啡

21 creamer (n.) 奶精

22 sugar (n.) 糖

23 tea (n.) 茶、紅茶
(= black tea / English tea)

24 green tea (n.) 綠茶

Useful Expressions
實用短句

1

需要呼叫空服員時，你可以說：

1 **Excuse me.**　　　　　　　　　　不好意思。

2

供應飲料時常用的短句：

1 **May I have another cup of coffee, please?**　　可以再給我一杯咖啡嗎？

2 **No ice, please.**　　　　　　　　請不要（給我）冰塊。

3 **Two sugar, please.**　　　　　　請給我兩塊糖。

4 **Do you have any hot drinks?**　　有熱飲嗎？

5 **Can I have some water?**　　　　可以給我水嗎？

6 **Just creamer, please.**　　　　　請（給我）奶精就好。

3

供應餐點時常用的短句：

1 **You don't have to wake me up for meals.**　　吃飯時請不用叫我起來。

2 **Could I have my meal later?**　　能否等等再幫我上餐？

Grammar 文法

01 Can I have ...? 能否給我……？

例 Can I have a glass of sparkling wine? 能給我一杯氣泡酒嗎？
Can I have some hot drinks? 能給我些熱飲嗎？

02 ..., please. 請給我某個食物或飲料。

例 Beer, please. 請給我啤酒。
Fish, please. 請給我魚肉。

03 使用 yes、no 的禮貌回答方式

例 Yes, please. 是的／好的，請給我。
No, thank you. 不用／不需要，謝謝。

04 Would you like 名詞？ 你想要／需要……嗎？（禮貌用法）

例 Would you like some water? 需要來點水嗎？
Would you like something to drink (or eat)? 您需要喝點什麼或吃點什麼嗎？

05 What kind of 名詞 do you ...? ……哪些種類的（東西）呢？

例 What kind of drinks do you have? 有哪些飲料可以選？
What kind of meat do you like? 你想要哪種肉呢？

一、生詞填空：請將適當的生詞填入空格中。

finished / bread / noodles / ice / white / tray / beverage / service

1. May I have another glass of _____ wine?

2. We ate chicken _____ for lunch.

3. Can I have a _____ menu?

4. Did you enjoy our _____?

5. One apple juice without _____, please.

6. May I please have some more _____?

7. Are you _____ with the meal?

8. Could you take away this _____?

二、問答：請用英語回答下列問題。

1. 如果想再要一杯啤酒的時候，該怎麼說？

_____

2. 被問到比較想吃魚肉或雞肉時，可以如何回答？

_____

3. 想問有什麼飲料時，該怎麼問？

_____

4. 想知道有沒有熱飲時，該怎麼問？

_____

三、文法填空：請將適當的句型填入空格中。

Are you finished / Which one would you like / please / What kind of
No, thank you / here's / Would you like / Do you need

A: We have chicken noodles and fish with rice. ① _____ to eat?

B: Chicken, ② _____ .

A: Here you are. ③ _____ something to drink?

B: ④ _____ drinks do you have?

A: We have juice, cola, beer, wine, and water.

B: Juice, ⑤ _____ .

A: Orange juice or apple juice?

B: Apple juice, please.

A: ⑥ _____ some ice?

B: ⑦ _____ .

A: ⑧ _____ with the meal?

B: Yes, ⑨ _____ my tray.

四、聽寫：請聽音檔，並將答案填入空格中。　　　　　　　　　mp3-06

A: We have chicken noodles and fish with rice. Which one would you like to eat?

B: ① _____

A: Here you are. Would you like something to drink?

B: ② _____

A: We have juice, cola, beer, wine, and water.

B: ③ _____

_____

A: Would you like some coffee or tea?

B: ④ _____

A: Would you like some lemon and sugar?

B: ⑤ _____

_____

A: Are you finished with the meal?

B: ⑥ _____

第二課 練習解答‧中文翻譯

一、生詞填空：請將適當的生詞填入空格中。

1. May I have another glass of **white** wine?
   可以再給我一杯白酒嗎？

2. We ate chicken **noodles** for lunch.
   我們午餐吃了雞肉麵。

3. Can I have a **beverage** menu?
   可以給我飲料菜單嗎？

4. Did you enjoy our **service**?
   您喜歡我們的服務嗎？

5. One apple juice without **ice**, please.
   請給我一杯蘋果汁不含冰塊。

6. May I please have some more **bread**?
   可以再給我一些麵包嗎？

7. Are you **finished** with the meal?
   您吃完了嗎？

8. Could you take away this **tray**?
   可以收走這個托盤嗎？

二、問答：請用英語回答下列問題。

1. **May I have one more beer?**　　　　　可以再給我一杯啤酒嗎？

2. **Fish, please.**　　　　　請給我魚肉。

3. **What kind of drinks do you have?**　　　　　有什麼種類的飲料？

4. **Do you have any hot drinks?**　　　　　有任何熱飲嗎？

三、文法填空：請將適當的句型填入空格中。

A: We have chicken noodles and fish with rice. ① **Which one would you like** to eat?

B: Chicken, ② **please**.

A: Here you are. ③ **Would you like** something to drink?

B: ④ **What kind of** drinks do you have?

A: We have juice, cola, beer, wine, and water.

B: Juice, ⑤ **please**.

A: Orange juice or apple juice?

B: Apple juice, please.

A: ⑥ **Do you need** some ice?

B: ⑦ **No, thank you**.

_____

A: ⑧ **Are you finished** with the meal?

B: Yes, ⑨ **here's** my tray.

中文翻譯

A：我們有雞肉麵跟魚肉飯，您想要吃哪個？
B：請給我雞肉（麵）。
A：這個給您。請問您需要喝點什麼嗎？
B：有什麼種類的飲料？
A：我們有果汁、可樂、啤酒、葡萄酒，還有水。
B：請給我果汁。
A：柳橙汁還是蘋果汁呢？
B：請給我蘋果汁。
A：您需要些冰塊嗎？
B：不用，謝謝。

A：您吃完了嗎？

B：是的，托盤給你。

四、聽寫：請聽音檔，並將答案填入空格中。

A: We have chicken noodles and fish with rice. Which one would you like to eat?

B: ① **Chicken, please.**

A: Here you are. Would you like something to drink?

B: ② **What kind of drinks do you have?**

A: We have juice, cola, beer, wine, and water.

B: ③ **Beer, please.**

A: Would you like some coffee or tea?

B: ④ **Tea, please.**

A: Would you like some lemon and sugar?

B: ⑤ **No, thank you.**

A: Are you finished with the meal?

B: ⑥ **Yes, here's my tray.**

中文翻譯

A：我們有雞肉麵跟魚肉飯，您想要吃哪個？

B：請給我雞肉（麵）。

A：這個給您。請問您需要喝點什麼嗎？

B：有什麼種類的飲料？

A：我們有果汁、可樂、啤酒、酒，還有水。

B：請給我啤酒。

A：需要來點咖啡或茶嗎？

B：請給我茶。

A：需要檸檬和糖嗎？

B：不用，謝謝。

A：您吃完了嗎？

B：是的，托盤給你。

What Happens During the Flight
飛行中的大小事

mp3-07

Dialogue A: Feeling Sick
(A: Flight attendant / B: Passenger 1 / C: Passenger 2)

A Is everything all right, sir.

B I am not feeling well.

A Would you like any medicine?

B Yes. Do you have any airsickness pills?

A Yes, we do. Would you like any blankets and pillows, too?

B Yes, please. Also, may I have a bottled water?

A OK. I will bring them to you right away.

B May I recline my seat?

C Sure. Go ahead.

Chinese Translation
中文翻譯

會話A：感覺生病了
（A：空服員 / B：乘客一 / C：乘客二）

A：先生，一切都還好嗎？
B：我感覺不太舒服。
A：您要吃點藥嗎？
B：好。你有暈機藥嗎？
A：有，我們有。您還想要毯子和枕頭嗎？
B：好，請給我。另外，可以給我一瓶瓶裝水嗎？
A：當然，我會馬上把它們帶給您。
B：我可以把座椅向後仰嗎？
C：當然。做吧。

Dialogue B: Duty-Free Shopping
(A: Flight attendant / B: Passenger)

B *(points to an item on the duty-free catalogue)* May I see this watch?

A Yes, here you go.

B Do you take credit cards?

A Yes. We accept most major credit cards. Also, you can pay in cash. We accept both Taiwanese dollars and US dollars.

Chinese Translation
中文翻譯

會話B：免稅購物
（A：空服員 / B：乘客）

B：（將手指向目錄上的圖片）我可以看一下這隻手錶嗎？

A：當然，這給您。

B：你接受信用卡嗎？

A：是的。我們接受大多數主要的信用卡。您也可以用現金支付。我們接受新台幣和美金。

mp3-08

❶ feel (v.) 感覺；覺得

❷ medicine (n.) 藥、藥品

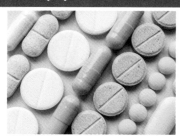

❸ airsickness (n.) 暈機

❹ blanket (n.) 毛毯、毯子

❺ pillow (n.) 枕頭

❻ bottled (adj.) 瓶裝的

❼ right away 立刻、馬上

❽ recline (v.) 使斜倚；使後仰

⑨ seat (n.) 座、座位

⑩ go ahead （用於給別人許可）進行、開始做

⑪ watch (n.) 錶、手錶

⑫ credit card (n.) 信用卡

⑬ accept (v.) 接受

⑭ major (adj.) 主要的、重大的

⑮ cash (n.) 現金

Useful Expressions
實用短句

1

當你想要某件物品時，你可以說：

1 Could you get me a pillow and a blanket, please?   可以請您給我一個枕頭和毯子嗎？

2 May I have another blanket?   我可以再要一條毯子嗎？

3 Could you bring me a magazine?   您能帶本雜誌給我嗎？

4 Can I have some water without ice?   我可以要不含冰塊的水嗎？

5 I need an airsickness bag, please.   請給我一個嘔吐袋。

2

當你覺得不舒服的時候，你可以說：

1 I do not feel very well.   我感覺不太舒服。

2 I feel a little sick.   我覺得有點生病了。

3 I feel like I am about to vomit.   我覺得我好像要吐了。

4 My ears are ringing.   我有耳鳴。

3

有關座位的短句：

1 May I recline my seat?   我可以將我的座椅向後仰嗎？

2 May I get through?   我可以通過嗎？

3 Would you mind changing seats?   您介意更換座位嗎？

4 May I move over there?   我可以移動到那裡嗎？

4 其他在飛機上常用的短句：

1 **Could you please put my bag into the overhead compartment?** 　您能幫把我的包包放到頭頂上的行李置物櫃裡嗎？

2 **Could you please help me get my bag out?** 　您能幫我拿出我的包包嗎？

3 **Can I use the restroom now?** 　我現在可以使用廁所嗎？

4 **What is the local time?** 　當地時間是幾點？

01 I feel ... 我覺得……

例 I feel hot / cold / chilly. 　　　　　　　　　我覺得熱／冷／寒冷。

I feel sick / sore / dizzy / sleepy / comfortable. 我覺得生病了／痠痛／頭暈／想睡／舒適。

I feel happy / sad / angry / good / bad. 　　　我覺得高興／難過／生氣／心情好／內疚。

It is time to eat. I feel hungry. 　　　　　　吃飯時間到了，我覺得好餓。

02 also 又、也、並且

例 I bought lipsticks and also perfumes. 　　　我買了口紅，也買了香水。

Taiwanese food is really great. Also, some Japanese meals in Taiwan are nice, too. 　　台灣菜真的很棒。另外，台灣的一些日本料理也很不錯。

03 Sure. Go ahead. （允許他人行動）當然，去做吧。

例 A: Can I ask you some personal questions? 　A：我可以問你一些私人問題嗎？

B: Sure. Go ahead. 　　　　　　　　　　　　B：當然可以，問吧。

A: Can I use the restroom first? 　　　　　　A：我可以先用廁所嗎？

B: Sure. Go ahead. 　　　　　　　　　　　　B：當然可以，用吧。

04 bring A to B = bring B A 把 A 帶（拿）給 B

例 I will bring some water to you. = I will bring you some water.

我會拿些水給你。＝我會拿給你一些水。

Could you bring a newspaper to me? = Could you bring me a newspaper?

你可以帶份報紙給我嗎？＝你可以給我一份報紙嗎？

05 both A and B 既 A 又 B；A 和 B 兩個都

例 He can speak both English and Japanese.　　他既會說英語又會說日語。

This bag is both good and cheap.　　這個包包既好又便宜。

一、生詞填空：請將適當的生詞填入空格中。

> blankets / major / right away / reclining / pillows / airsickness / feel / accept

1. I _____ sleepy.

2. Do you need some medicine for _____ ?

3. I need soft _____ to have a good night's sleep.

4. We cannot _____ your request.

5. It's good weather today. Let's wash the _____ .

6. I will call them _____ .

7. You should ask for permission before _____ your airplane seat.

8. Traffic jam is a _____ urban problem.

二、問答：請用英語回答下列問題。

1. 當有耳鳴時，你要如何表達？

_____

2. 當要去洗手間時，須經過鄰座。你要怎麼表達？

_____

3. 你想問當地時間時，該怎麼說？

_____

4. 當想再要一條毯子時，你該怎麼說？

_____

Lesson 3 | 第三課

三、文法填空：請將適當的句型填入空格中。

> Would you like / most major / may I have / Sure / here you go
> Do you take / Go ahead / Do you have / all right

A: Is everything ① _____ , sir?

B: I am not feeling well.

A: Would you like any medicine?

B: Yes. ② _____ any airsickness medicine?

A: Yes, we do. ③ _____ any blankets and pillows?

B: Yes, please. Also, ④ _____ a bottled water?

A: OK. I will bring them to you right away.

B: May I recline my seat?

C: ⑤ _____ . ⑥ _____ .

B: May I see this watch?

A: Yes, ⑦ _____ .

B: ⑧ _____ credit cards?

A: Yes. We accept ⑨ _____ credit cards.

A: Is everything all right, sir?

B: ① _____

A: Would you like any medicine?

B: ② _____

A: Yes, we do. Would you like any blankets and pillows?

B: ③ _____

A: OK, then I will bring the medicine to you right away.

B: May I recline my seat?

C: ④ _____

――――――――――――――――――――――――――――

B: ⑤ _____

A: Yes, here you go.

B: ⑥ _____

A: Yes, you can. You can also pay in New Taiwan dollars.

第三課 練習解答・中文翻譯

一、生詞填空：請將適當的生詞填入空格中。

1. I **feel** sleepy.
   我覺得睏。

2. Do you need some medicine for **airsickness**?
   你需要些改善暈機的藥嗎？

3. I need soft **pillows** to have a good night's sleep.
   我需要軟的枕頭，才能睡個好覺。

4. We cannot **accept** your request.
   我們不能接受你的要求。

5. It's good weather today. Let's wash the **blankets**.
   今天是好天氣。我們來洗毯子吧。

6. I will call them **right away**.
   我會馬上打電話給他們。

7. You should ask for permission before **reclining** your airplane seat.
   你應該徵得同意後，再把飛機座椅向後仰。

8. Traffic jam is a **major** urban problem.
   塞車是一個很大的都市問題。

二、問答：請用英語回答下列問題。

1. **My ears are ringing.**　　　　　　　　　我正在耳鳴。

2. **May I get through?**　　　　　　　　　　我可以通過嗎？

3. **What's the local time?**　　　　　　　　當地時間是幾點？

4. **May I have another blanket?**　　　　　　我可以再有一件毛毯嗎？

三、文法填空：請將適當的句型填入空格中。

A: Is everything ① **all right**, sir?

B: I am not feeling well.

A: Would you like any medicine?

B: Yes. ② **Do you have** any airsickness medicine?

A: Yes, we do. ③ **Would you like** any blankets and pillows?

B: Yes, please. Also, ④ **may I have** a bottled water?

A: OK. I will bring them to you right away.

B: May I recline my seat?

A: ⑤ **Sure.** ⑥ **Go ahead.**

B: May I see this watch?

A: Yes, ⑦ **here you go.**

B: ⑧ **Do you take** credit cards?

A: Yes. We accept ⑨ **most major** credit cards.

中文翻譯請見 P. 41,43。

四、聽寫：請聽音檔，並將答案填入空格中。

A: Is everything all right, sir?

B: ① **I am feeling a little sick.**

A: Would you like any medicine?

B: ② **Yes. Do you have any airsickness medicine?**

A: Yes, we do. Would you like any blankets and pillows?

B: ③ **No, thank you.**

A: OK, then I will bring the medicine to you right away.

B: May I recline my seat?

C: ④ **Sure. Go ahead.**

B: ⑤ **May I see this lipstick?**

A: Yes, here you go.

B: ⑥ **Can I pay in dollars?**

A: Yes, you can. You can also pay in New Taiwan dollars.

中文翻譯

A：先生，一切都還好嗎？

B：我覺得有點想吐。

A：您要吃點藥嗎？

B：好。你有任何暈機藥嗎？

A：是的，我們有。您還想要毯子和枕頭嗎？

B：不用，謝謝你。

A：好的。我會馬上把藥帶給您。

B：我可以把我的座椅向後仰嗎？

C：當然。做吧。

B：我可以看一下這個口紅嗎？

A：可以，這給您。

B：我可以付美金嗎？

A：可以。您也可以付新台幣。

Dialogue A: Passport Inspection
(A: Immigration officer / B: Traveler)

A What is the purpose of your visit?

B Sightseeing.

A Are you traveling alone?

B No, I came with my sister.

A How long will you be staying in this country?

B I will be here for a week.

A Where are you going to stay?

B I have booked ABC hotel in Brisbane.

Chinese Translation
中文翻譯

會話A：護照查驗
（A：移民官 / B：旅客）

A：您入境的目的是什麼？
B：觀光。
A：您是獨自旅遊嗎？
B：不是，我和我姐姐一起來。
A：您會在這個國家停留多久的時間？
B：我會在這裡一週。
A：您會住在哪裡呢？
B：我已經訂了布里斯本的 ABC 飯店。

Dialogue B: Going through Customs
(A: Customs officer / B: Traveler)

A Do you have any meat products, fruits or vegetables in your luggage?

B No, I do not.

A Do you have anything to declare?

B Yes, I have two cartons of cigarettes. Do I need to pay extra?

A Yes. You are only allowed one carton tax-free, so you have to pay $25 for the extra carton.

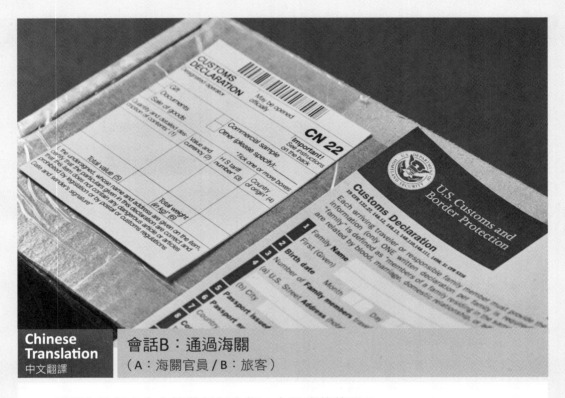

Chinese Translation
中文翻譯

會話B：通過海關
（A：海關官員 / B：旅客）

A：請問您的行李中有攜帶任何肉類、水果或蔬菜嗎？

B：不，我沒有。

A：請問您有任何東西需要申報嗎？

B：有的，我有兩條香菸。請問我需要額外付費嗎？

A：是的。您只能攜帶一條免稅的香菸，所以您必須要為額外的那一條多付美金 25 元。

mp3-11

1 inspection (n.) 檢查

2 purpose (n.) 目的

3 visit (n. / v.) 拜訪、來訪

4 sightseeing (n.) 觀光

5 alone (adv.) 獨自、一個人

6 country (n.) 國家

7 stay (n. / v.) 停留、住宿

8 book (v.) 預訂

⑨ product (n.) 產品、商品

⑩ fruit (n.) 水果

⑪ vegetable (n.) 蔬菜

⑫ declare (n.) 申報

⑬ carton (n.) 紙盒、紙箱；一條菸（一般含有 10 包）

⑭ cigarette (n.) 香菸

⑮ pay (v.) 付款

⑯ extra (adj.) 額外的

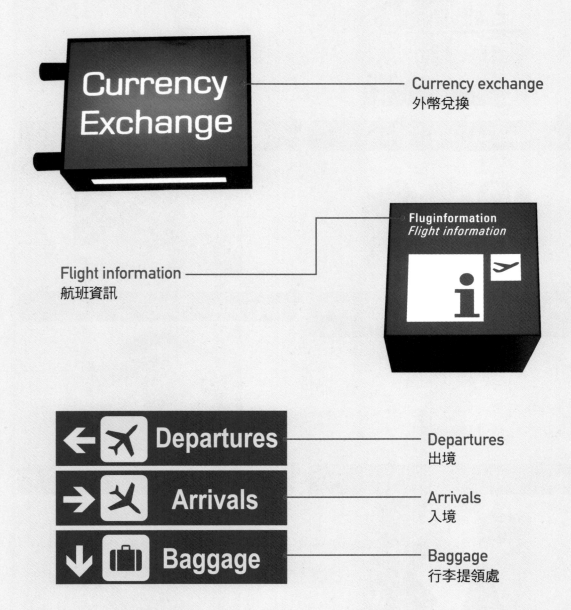

Currency exchange
外幣兌換

Fluginformation
Flight information

Flight information
航班資訊

Departures
出境

Arrivals
入境

Baggage
行李提領處

Transfer
轉機

Ticketing / Check-in
票務／報到

Bag Claim
行李提領處

Parking
停車場

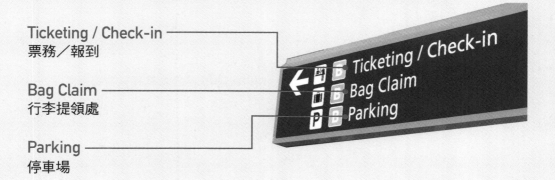

Immigration
入境查驗

VAT refunds
退稅

1

入關時海關人員常問的問題：

1 What is the purpose of your visit? 　請問您來訪的目的是什麼？

你可以回答：

Sightseeing.	觀光。
Business.	出差。
To study.	讀書。
On vacation.	旅遊。

2 How long will you be staying in this country? 　您會在這裡停留多久？

你可以回答：

I will be here for a week.	我會停留一週。
3 Days.	三天。

3 Where are you going to stay? 　您會住在哪裡？

你可以回答：

I have booked Gloria hotel in Taipei.	我已經預訂了台北的葛洛莉旅館。
I am staying at Gloria hotel.	我會住在的葛洛莉旅館。
I will stay at my friend's place.	我會住在我朋友家。

4 Is this your first time to 國名？ 　這是你第一次來到某國家嗎？

你可以回答：

Yes, this is my first time here.	是的，這是我第一次來這裡。
No, this is my second / third / forth time here.	不是，這是我第二／三／四次來這裡。

5 Do you have anything to declare?　　請問您有任何物品需要申報嗎？

你可以回答：

Yes, I do.　　　　　　　　　　是的，我有。

No, I do not.　　　　　　　　　不，我沒有。

Nothing.　　　　　　　　　　　沒有。

No. I have nothing to declare.　　不，我沒有東西要申報。

Grammar 文法

01 be 動詞＋現在分詞（動詞 ing 形） （用現在進行式表示未來的計劃）要⋯⋯

例 I am leaving soon.　　　　　　　　　　　我要離開了。

Are you buying this?　　　　　　　　　　您要買這個嗎？

02 have ＋過去分詞（動詞 p.p. 形） （現在完成式）已經⋯⋯

例 I have lost my passport.　　　　　　　　我遺失我的護照了。

He told me his name but I have forgotten.　他告訴過我他的名字，但是我忘記了。

03 need to ＋動詞原形 需要⋯⋯

例 Do I need to fill out this form?　　　　　我需要填這個表格嗎？

I need to take medicine after meals.　　　我需要在用餐後吃藥。

04 You are allowed ＋名詞 你可以⋯⋯（你被允許有某件物品）

You are allowed to ＋動詞原形 你可以⋯⋯（你被允許去做某件事）

例 You are allowed a visa-free stay.　　　　你可以免簽證停留。

You are only allowed one piece of luggage.　你只能帶一件行李。

You are not allowed to go out after 10pm.　你不可以在晚上 10 點後外出。

05 have to ＋動詞原形 必須⋯⋯

例 I have to pay this bill today.　　　　　　我今天必須付帳單。

I have to book a hotel before Monday.　　我必須在星期一之前預訂一間飯店。

06 數量＋ carton(s) of ＋名詞 ～ （紙）盒／條／箱的～

例 I have one carton of cigarettes.　　　　　　我有一箱的香菸。

　　I bought three cartons of milk.　　　　　　我買了三盒牛奶。

Exercise 練習

一、生詞填空：請將適當的生詞填入空格中。

> purpose / declare / book / product / sightseeing
> alone / extra / inspection

1. This restaurant is very popular, so we need to ⬚⬚⬚⬚⬚⬚ a table in advance.

2. I went to Japan ⬚⬚⬚⬚⬚⬚ last week.

3. This is a good place for ⬚⬚⬚⬚⬚⬚ .

4. We went for a drive without any ⬚⬚⬚⬚⬚⬚ .

5. Do you need an ⬚⬚⬚⬚⬚⬚ blanket?

6. Police asked me to show them a car license for ⬚⬚⬚⬚⬚⬚ .

7. I do not have anything to ⬚⬚⬚⬚⬚⬚ at the customs.

8. This new ⬚⬚⬚⬚⬚⬚ sold out in one day.

二、問答：請用英語回答下列問題。

1. 當你被問到來訪的目的，而你的目的是觀光時，你會如何回答？

_____

2. 當你被問到會在這個國家停留多久，而你預定停留 10 天時，你會如何回答？

_____

3. 當你想確認是否需要額外付費，你會如何詢問？

_____

4. 當你被問到是否有任何物品需要申報，而你是沒有需要時，你會如何回答？

_____

三、文法填空：請將適當的句型填入空格中。

> **Where will you be / Do you have / in / What is the purpose of / have to**
> **I have booked / Do I need to / How long / Are you**

A: ① _____ your visit?

B: Sightseeing.

A: ② _____ traveling alone?

B: No, I came with my sister.

A: ③ _____ will you stay?

B: I will be here for a week.

A: ④ _____ staying in this country?

C: ⑤ _____ ABC hotel ⑥ _____ Brisbane.

A: ⑦ _____ any meat products, fruits or vegetables in your luggage?

B: No, I don't.

A: ⑧ _____ anything to declare?

B: Yes, I have two cartons of cigarettes. ⑨ _____ pay extra?

A: Yes. You're only allowed one carton tax-free, so you ⑩ _____ pay $25 for the extra carton.

四、聽寫：請聽音檔，並將答案填入空格中。

A: What is the purpose of your visit?

B: ① _____

A: Are you traveling alone?

B: ② _____

A: How long will you be staying in this country?

B: ③ _____

A: Where will you stay?

B: ④ _____

_____

A: Do you have any meat products, fruits or vegetables in your luggage?

B: ⑤ _____

A: Do you have anything to declare?

B: ⑥ _____

第四課 練習解答 · 中文翻譯

一、生詞填空：請將適當的生詞填入空格中。

1. This restaurant is very popular, so we need to **book** a table in advance.
   這家餐廳很受歡迎，因此我們需要提前預定座位。

2. I went to Japan **alone** last week.
   我上週獨自去了日本。

3. This is a good place for **sightseeing**.
   這裡是觀光的好地方。

4. We went for a drive without any **purpose**.
   我們開車兜風去了，沒有任何目的。

5. Do you need an **extra** blanket?
   您需要額外的毯子嗎？

6. Police asked me to show them a car license for **inspection**.
   警方要求我出示駕照以供查驗。

7. I do not have anything to **declare** at the customs.
   我沒有什麼要向海關申報的。

8. This new **product** sold out in one day.
   這種新的產品已在一天內售罄。

二、問答：請用英語回答下列問題。

1. **Sightseeing.** 觀光。

2. **I will be here for 10 days.** 我會在這裡十天。

3. **Do I need to pay extra?** 請問我需要額外付費嗎？

4. **No, I don't.** 不，我沒有。

三、文法填空：請將適當的句型填入空格中。

A: ① **What is the purpose of** your visit?

B: Sightseeing.

A: ② **Are you** traveling alone?

B: No, I came with my sister.

A: ③ **How long** will you stay?

B: I will be here for a week.

A: ④ **Where will you be** staying in this country?

B: ⑤ **I have booked** ABC hotel ⑥ **in** Brisbane.

B: ⑦ **Do you have** any meat products, fruits or vegetables in your luggage?

A: No, I don't.

A: ⑧ **Do you have** anything to declare?

B: Yes, I have two cartons of cigarettes. ⑨ **Do I need to** pay extra?

A: Yes. You're only allowed one carton tax-free, so you ⑩ **have to** pay $25 for the extra carton.

中文翻譯請見 **P. 57,59**。

四、聽寫：請聽音檔，並將答案填入空格中。

A: What is the purpose of your visit?

B: ① **Business.**

A: Are you traveling alone?

B: ② **Yes, I am.**

A: How long will you be staying in this country?

B: ③ **I will be here for 4 days.**

A: Where will you stay?

B: ④ **I am staying at Blue hotel.**

A: Do you have any meat products, fruits or vegetables in your luggage?

B: ⑤ **No, I don't.**

A: Do you have anything to declare?

B: ⑥ **No. I have nothing to declare.**

中文翻譯

A：您來訪的目的是什麼？

B：出差。

A：請問您是獨自旅遊嗎？

B：是的，我是。

A：您會在這個國家停留多久的時間？

B：我會在這裡四天。

A：您會住在哪裡呢？

B：我會住在藍色旅館。

A：請問您的行李中有攜帶任何肉類、水果或蔬菜嗎？

B：沒有。

A：請問您有任何東西需要申報嗎？

B：不，我沒有東西要申報。

Lesson 5 | 第五課 | Currency Exchange
換匯

 **Dialogue 會話**

mp3-13

Dialogue A: At the Currency Exchange Counter
(A: Customer / B: Staff)

A I'd like to change my money into US dollars.

B Which currency would you like to exchange?

A New Taiwan dollars into US dollars. What is the exchange rate today?

B It's 1 to 0.033.

A I see.

B How much would you like to exchange?

A I would like to exchange 30,000 New Taiwan dollars.

B Certainly.

A How much is the commission?

B We charge a one-dollar commission per transaction.

A OK.

B How would you like your bills?

A Ten twenties, twenty tens and the rest in singles, please.

B Here is your money.

A May I have a receipt, please?

B Sure. I will print one out for you.

Chinese Translation
中文翻譯

會話A：在換匯櫃檯
（A：客戶 / B：櫃員）

A：我想要將我的錢換成美元。

B：您想兌換哪種貨幣？

A：新台幣兌美元。今天的匯率是多少？

B：是 1 比 0.033。

A：我明白了。

B：您想換多少錢？

A：我想換新台幣 30,000 元。

B：沒問題。

A：佣金是多少？

B：我們每筆交易收取一美元的佣金。

A：好的。

B：您想要哪些面額？

A：請給我 10 張二十元、20 張十元，其餘的都換一元紙幣。

B：這是您的錢。

A：可以給我一張收據嗎？

B：沒問題。我會為您印一張出來。

① exchange rate 匯率

② commission (n.) 佣金

handling fee 手續費、transaction fee 交易費

③ transaction (n.) 交易、辦理

④ receipt (n.) 收據

⑤ rest (n.) 其餘的

⑥ print ... out 印出來

Foreign Currency 外國貨幣

US dollar (USD) 美金

bill 紙鈔

coin 硬幣

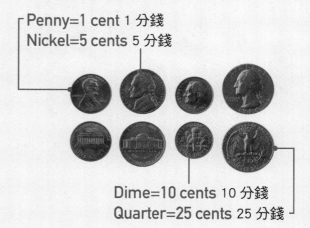

Penny=1 cent 1 分錢
Nickel=5 cents 5 分錢

Dime=10 cents 10 分錢
Quarter=25 cents 25 分錢

Australian dollar 澳幣

Euro 歐元

New Taiwan dollar (NTD) 新台幣

Japanese yen 日幣

1

想要換匯時，你可以說：

1 **Exchange, please.**　　　　　　請幫我換匯。

2 **Can I exchange New Taiwan dollar for US dollar?**　　　我可以將新台幣換成美元嗎？

3 **Can I exchange New Taiwan dollar for local currency?**　　　我可以將新台幣換成當地的貨幣嗎？

2

想要詢問匯率時，你可以說：

1 **What is the current exchange rate from New Taiwan dollar to US dollar?**　　　新台幣對美元的當前匯率是多少？

3

想要詢問費用，你可以說：

1 **How much commission do you charge?**　　　你收取多少佣金？

2 **How much is the handling fee?**　　　手續費是多少？

4

在換匯的過程中，承辦人員可能會問你：

1 **How much would you like to exchange?**　　　您想要換多少錢？

2 **How would you like your bills?**　　　您想要兌換哪些面額？

5 想要指定兌換細節時，你可以說：

1 I would like it in ten-dollar bills, please.　　請給我十美元的紙幣。

2 Can I have some small change?　　可以給我些零錢嗎？

3 All in twenty-dollar bills, please.　　請全部給我二十美元的紙幣。

4 Can I change my 100 US dollars to 5 twenty-dollar bills?　　我可以將 100 美元換成 5 張二十美元面額的紙幣嗎？

6 其他換匯相關的常用短句：

1 Where can I exchange the money?　　我可以去哪裡換匯？

2 Could you deal with New Taiwan dollars?　　（我）能用新台幣跟您交易嗎？

3 Could you break this 100-dollar bill?　　您可以把這張 100 美元的紙幣換成零錢嗎？

Grammar
文法

01 change A into B = exchange A for B 將貨幣 A 換成貨幣 B

例 Could you change New Taiwan dollar
into Japanese yen?　　　　　　　　您能將新台幣換成日圓嗎？

I would like to change this into dollars.　我想把這個換成美元。

02 A to B 匯率的表示方法

例 A: I'd like to exchange New Taiwan dollars　我想將新台幣兌換成美元。請問匯率是多少？
for US dollars. What is the exchange rate?

B: It's 1 to 0.33.　　　　　　　　　　是 1 比 0.33。

03 per 每～

例 How much is the tour per person?　　　這個旅遊行程每人會收多少錢？

Your wage is NTD250 per hour.　　　　您的時薪為每小時新台幣 250 元。

04 in ＋貨幣 幣別的表示方法

例 Can I pay in New Taiwan dollars?　　　我可以用新台幣付款嗎？

How much is that in US dollars?　　　　那個用美元算的話是多少錢？

05 in ＋面額 面額的表示方法

例 in singles / in tens / in twenties / in fifties / in hundred-dollar bills
　1 元／ 10 元／ 20 元／ 50 元／ 100 元的面額

A: How would you like your money?　　　您的錢要兌換成何種面額？

B: Five in twenties and the rest in　　　請給我 5 張二十元（紙幣），其餘的請都換
hundred-dollar bills, please.　　　　　成百元紙鈔。

一、生詞填空：請將適當的生詞填入空格中。

> bills / receipt / commission / exchange rate
> transactions / rest / tens / dollars

1. Here's your credit card and _____ .

2. I would like to change my money into _____ .

3. When you exchange money, you'll have to pay _____ of around 1%.

4. Do you wish to make any other _____ ?

5. I would like to change this fifty-dollar bill into _____ .

6. I gave my brother two five-dollar _____ .

7. I will love you for the _____ of my life.

8. What is the current _____ from New Taiwan dollar to Japanese yen?

二、問答：請用英語回答下列問題。

1. 當對方想問你今天新台幣對美元的匯率是多少時，他會如何表達？

_____

2. 當想用新台幣兌換美元時，你該如何表達？

_____

3. 想問對方是否接受用新台幣交易時，你該說什麼句子？

_____

4. 對方想將持有的一百元美鈔換成零錢時，他會如何表達？

_____

5. 換匯時，若希望將所有的錢都換成面額二十元的美鈔，你該說什麼句子？

_____

三、文法填空：請將適當的句型填入空格中。

> What is / in / Certainly / How would you like
> How much / change … into / print … out / into

A: I'd like to ① _____ my money _____ dollars.

B: What currency would you like to exchange?

A: New Taiwan dollars ② _____ US dollars. ③ _____ the exchange rate today?

B: It's 1 to 0.033.

A: I see.

B: How much would you like to exchange?

A: I would like to exchange 30,000 New Taiwan dollars.

B: ④ _____ .

A: ⑤ _____ is the commission?

B: We charge a one-dollar commission transaction.

A: OK.

B: ⑥ _____ your bills?

A: Ten twenties, twenty tens and the rest ⑦ _____ singles, please.

B: Here is your money.

A: May I have a receipt, please?

B: Sure. I will ⑧ _____ one _____ for you.

四、聽寫：請聽音檔，並將答案填入空格中。

mp3-15

A: ① _____

B: What currency would you like to exchange?

A: New Taiwan dollars into US dollars. ② _____

B: It's 1 to 0.033.

A: I see.

B: How much would you like to exchange?

A: ③ _____

B: Certainly.

A: ④ _____

B: We charge a one-dollar commission per transaction.

A: OK.

B: How would you like your bills?

A: ⑤ _____, please.

B: Here is your money.

A: ⑥ _____, please?

B: Sure. I will print one out for you.

第五課 練習解答．中文翻譯

一、生詞填空：請將適當的生詞填入空格中。

1. Here's your credit card and **receipt**.
   這是您的信用卡和收據。

2. I would like to change my money into **dollars**.
   我想把我的錢換成美元。

3. When you exchange money, you'll have to pay **commission** of around 1%.
   換匯時，您將必須支付大約 1% 的佣金。

4. Do you wish to make any other **transactions**?
   您是否還想進行其他交易？

5. I would like to change this fifty-dollar bill into **tens**.
   我想把這五十元的鈔票換成十元的。

6. I gave my brother two five-dollar **bills**.
   我給了我哥哥 2 張五元鈔票。

7. I will love you for the **rest** of my life.
   我的餘生都會愛你。

8. What is the current **exchange rate** from New Taiwan dollar to Japanese yen?
   新台幣對日幣的當前匯率是多少？

二、問答：請用英語回答下列問題。

1. **What is the current exchange rate from New Taiwan dollar to US dollar?**　　新台幣對美元的當前匯率是多少？

2. **I would like to change New Taiwan dollars into US dollars.**　　我想把新台幣換成美元。

3. **Do you accept New Taiwan dollars?**　　你接受新台幣嗎？

4. **Could you break this hundred-dollar bill?**　　你可以把這張 100 美元的鈔票換成零錢嗎？

5. **All in twenty-dollar bills, please.**　　請全部給我 20 元紙幣。

三、文法填空：請將適當的句型填入空格中。

A: I'd like to ① **change** my money **into** dollars.

B: What currency would you like to exchange?

A: New Taiwan dollars ② **into** US dollars. ③ **What is** the exchange rate today?

B: It's 1 to 0.033.

A: I see.

B: How much would you like to exchange?

A: I would like to exchange 30,000 New Taiwan dollars.

B: ④ **Certainly.**

A: ⑤ **How much** is the commission?

B: We charge a one-dollar commission transaction.

A: OK.

B: ⑥ **How would you like** your bills?

A: Ten twenties, twenty tens and the rest ⑦ **in** singles, please.

B: Here is your money.

A: May I have a receipt, please?

B: Sure. I will ⑧ **print** one **out** for you.

中文翻譯請見 P. 76-77。

四、聽寫：請聽音檔，並將答案填入空格中。

A: ① **I'd like to change my money into dollars.**

B: What currency would you like to exchange?

A: New Taiwan dollars into US dollars. ② **What is the exchange rate today?**

B: It's 1 to 0.033.

A: I see.

B: How much would you like to exchange?

A: ③ **I would like to exchange 30,000 New Taiwan dollars.**

B: Certainly.

A: ④ **How much is the commission?**

B: We charge a one-dollar commission per transaction.

A: OK.

B: How would you like your bills?

A: ⑤ **Ten twenties, twenty tens and the rest in singles**, please.

B: Here is your money.

A: ⑥ **May I have a receipt**, please?

B: Sure. I will print one out for you.

中文翻譯請見 P.76-77。

Checking-in at the Hotel
在飯店辦理入住手續

mp3-16

Dialogue A: I Would Like to Check-in.
(A: Front desk clerk / B: Guest)

A Good afternoon. How may I help you today?

B I would like to check-in.

A Certainly. Do you have a reservation?

B Yes, I do.

A Could you please give me your name?

B My name is Chen. This is the confirmation slip.

A Ms. Chen... yes, we have your reservation. Please fill out this registration form.

B OK.

A May I have your credit card for a deposit?

B Sure. Here you are.

A Great, thank you. Your room number is 403. It's on the fourth floor. Here is your room key.

B Thank you!

A Breakfast will be served from 7am to 9am on level B1. Please show your keycard to the staff.

B OK.

A If you have any requests, please call our front desk. Enjoy your stay.

Chinese Translation
中文翻譯

會話A：我想辦理入住。
（A：櫃檯人員／B：房客）

A：午安。我今天能為您提供什麼服務？
B：我想辦理入住。
A：沒問題。您有預約嗎？
B：是的，我有。
A：能給我您的大名嗎？
B：我姓陳，這是訂房確認單。
A：陳女士……好的，我們有您的預約（紀錄）。請您填寫這張住房登記表。
B：好的。
A：可以給我您的信用卡以支付押金嗎？
B：當然。這個給你。
A：好極了，謝謝。您的房號是 403。位於四樓。這是您的房間鑰匙。
B：謝謝。
A：早餐將從早上 7 點至早上 9 點在地下一樓提供。請向工作人員出示您的鑰

　　匙磁卡。

B：好的。

A：如果您有任何需求，請致電我們的櫃檯。祝您入住愉快。

mp3-17

❶ reservation (n.) 預約

❷ confirmation slip (n.) 確認單

❸ registration form (n.) 登記表

❹ deposit (n.) 押金

❺ floor (n.) 樓層

❻ fourth (adj.) 第四個的

❼ serve (v.) 服務

❽ basement (n.) 地下室；地下樓層

⑨ front desk (n.) 櫃檯

Types of Hotel Rooms 飯店房型

single room 單人房

double room 單床雙人房（一張雙人床）

twin room 雙床雙人房（兩張單人床）

family room 家庭房

How to Fill out a Registration Form 如何填寫住房登記表

First name
或 Forename 名字

Last name
或 Surname 姓氏

Address
居住地址

Zip code
或 postcode 郵遞區號

Telephone number
電話號碼

Title
（Mr.、Ms.、Mrs.、Dr. 等）稱謂

Nationality
國籍

Email
電子郵件

Leisure / Business
（指停留目的）休閒／商務

Signature
簽名（簽中文也可以喔！）

1

想要預約飯店房間時，你可以說：

1 I'd like to book a single / double / twin room for how many nights, please.

我想預約幾個晚上的一間單人房／單床雙人房／雙床雙人房。

例：**I'd like to book a double room for 3 nights, please.**

我想預約 3 個晚上的一間單床雙人房。

2 I'd like to make a reservation for a single / double / twin room on date.

我想預約幾月幾號的一間單人房 / 單床雙人房 / 雙床雙人房。

例：**I'd like to make a reservation for a twin room on July 11th.**

我想預約 7 月 11 日的一間雙床雙人房。

3 One single / double / twin room for how many nights, please.

請（給我）幾個晚上的一間單人房 / 單床雙人房 / 雙床雙人房。

例：**One single room for 2 nights, please.**

請（給我）2 個晚上的一間單人房。

2

到達飯店時，你可以向櫃檯人員說：

1 I have no reservation. Do you have any rooms available?

我沒有預約。你們還有空房嗎？

→依照情況，對方可能會給你不同的答覆：

(1) **Let me see…, yes, we do.**

讓我看看，是的，我們還有空房。

(2) **I'm afraid we're fully booked.**

不好意思，我們已經訂房全滿了。

(3) **Unfortunately, we have no rooms available.**

很遺憾，我們沒有空房間了。

2 I have a reservation under name.

我是姓名，我有預約。

例：**I have a reservation under Chen.**

我姓陳，我有預約。

3 想提出更多關於房型的請求時，你可以說：

1 May I have a (non) smoking room?

我可以住（非）吸菸房嗎？

2 Do you have any (non) smoking rooms available?

你們還有空的（非）吸菸房嗎？

3 Can we have a room with two separate beds?

我們房間可以有兩張分開的床嗎？

4 如果在可以辦理入住前，提早到達飯店，你可以問：

1 Can I use the room now?

我現在可以使用房間了嗎？

2 Can you keep my baggage until check-in time?

在可以辦理入住之前，你可以保管我的行李嗎？

5 其他在飯店裡常用的短句：

1 A: Could you spell your last name for me?

　　可以幫我拼出您的姓氏嗎？

B: Sure. It's C-H-E-N.

　　當然可以。拼法是 C-H-E-N。

2 Can I ask you to bring my baggage to my room?

　　我可以麻煩你把行李帶到我的房間嗎？

3 Is there free Wi-Fi in the room?

　　房間內有免費的 Wi-Fi（無線網路）嗎？

01 **Do you have ... available?** 有空的……嗎？

例 Do you have any rooms available? 你們有空房嗎？

Do you have any time available? 你有空閒（可供預約）的時段嗎？

02 **序數的寫法**

數字	序數	簡寫	數字	序數	簡寫
1	first	1st	11	eleventh	11th
2	second	2nd	12	twelfth	12th
3	third	3rd	13	thirteenth	13th
4	fourth	4th	14	fourteenth	14th
5	fifth	5th	15	fifteenth	15th
6	sixth	6th	16	sixteenth	16th
7	seventh	7th	17	seventeenth	17th
8	eighth	8th	18	eighteenth	18th
9	ninth	9th	19	nineteenth	19th
10	tenth	10th	20	twentieth	20th

03 **on the ＋序數＋ floor** 在第……層樓

例 Your room is located on the 4th floor. 你的房間位於第四層樓。

My room is on the second floor. 我的房間在第二層樓。

樓層	美式	英式
1 樓	first floor	ground floor
2 樓	second floor	first floor
3 樓	third floor	second floor

04 名詞 will be served. ……將被提供。

例 Coffee will be served after the meal.　餐後將提供咖啡。

Lunch will be served in an hour.　午餐將在一小時內提供。

05 If you have any 名詞 如果你有任何……

例 Please tell us if you have any questions.　如有任何問題，請告訴我們。

If you have any problems, let me know.　如果你有任何問題，請告訴我。

Exercise 練習

一、生詞填空：請將適當的生詞填入空格中。

> registration form / reservation / confirmation slip / postcode
> title / first name / deposit / floors

1. Please tell me how to fill out the ███████████ .
2. There are 23 ██████████████ in this hotel.
3. I would like to make a ███████████████ for 2 nights.
4. What is the █████████████ in your local area?
5. Could you tell me how to spell your ████████████████ ?
6. You have to pay a ████████████ to rent a car.
7. Please show me the ██████████████ and your passport.
8. The ███████████ "Mrs." means you are married.

二、問答：請用英語回答下列問題。

1. 如何詢問是否有空房？

_____

2. 當你想表示自己已經預約了 2 個晚上的一間單人房時，該怎麼說？

_____

3. 如果在可以辦理入住之前，你想請飯店幫忙保管行李，該如何詢問？

_____

4. 想知道房間中是否有免費的 Wi-Fi，該如何表達？

_____

三、文法填空：請將適當的句型填入空格中。

> be served / How may I / fill out / call / on the fourth
> Could you please / If you have / Here is

A: Good afternoon. ① _____ help you today?

B: I would like to check-in.

A: Certainly. Do you have a reservation?

B: Yes, I do.

A: ② _____ give me your name?

B: My name is Chen. This is the confirmation slip.

A: Ms. Chen. Yes, we have your reservation. Please ③ _____ this registration form.

B: OK.

A: May I have your credit card for a deposit?

B: Sure. Here you are.

A: Your room number is 403. It's ④ _____ floor. ⑤ _____ your room key.

B: Thank you.

A: Breakfast will ⑥ _____ from 7am to 9am on level B1. Please show your keycard to the staff.

B: OK.

A: ⑦ _____ any requests, please ⑧ _____ our front desk. Enjoy your stay.

四、聽寫：請聽音檔，並將答案填入空格中。 mp3-18

A: Good afternoon. How may I help you today?

B: ① _____

A: Certainly. Do you have a reservation?

B: Yes, I do.

A: Could you please give me your name?

B: My name is Chen. ② _____

A: Ms. Chen. Yes, we have your reservation. Please fill out this registration form.

B: OK.

A: May I have your credit card ③ _____

B: Sure. Here you are.

A: Your room number is 403. It's on the fourth floor.

　④ _____

B: Thank you.

A: Breakfast will be served from 7am to 9am ⑤ _____

　Please show your keycard to the staff.

B: OK.

A: ⑥ _____, please call our front desk. Enjoy your stay.

第六課 練習解答‧中文翻譯

一、生詞填空：請將適當的生詞填入空格中。

1. Please tell me how to fill out the **registration form**.
   請告訴我如何填寫登記表。

2. There are 23 **floors** in this hotel.
   這家飯店有 23 層。

3. I would like to make a **reservation** for 2 nights.
   我想預約兩晚的房間。

4. What is the **postcode** in your local area.
   你當地的郵遞區號是什麼？

5. Could you tell me how to spell your **first name**?
   您能告訴我如何拼寫您的名字嗎？

6. You have to pay a **deposit** to rent a car.
   您必須支付押金才能租車。

7. Please show me the **confirmation slip** and your passport.
   請出示訂房確認單和您的護照。

8. The **title** "Mrs." means you are married.
   「女士」的稱謂是指您已婚。

二、問答：請用英語回答下列問題。

1. **Do you have any rooms available?**   你們還有空房嗎？

2. **I've made a reservation for one single room for 2 nights.**   我已經預約了兩個晚上的一間單人房。

3. **Can you keep my baggage until check-in time?**   在可以辦理入住之前，你可以保管我的行李嗎？

4. **Is there free Wi-Fi in the room?**   房間內有免費的 Wi-Fi （無線網路）嗎？

三、文法填空：請將適當的句型填入空格中。

A: Good afternoon. ① **How may I** help you today?

B: I would like to check-in.

A: Certainly. Do you have a reservation?

B: Yes, I do.

A: ② **Could you please** give me your name?

B: My name is Chen. This is the confirmation slip.

A: Ms. Chen. Yes, we have your reservation. Please ③ **fill out** this registration form.

B: OK.

A: May I have your credit card for a deposit?

B: Sure. Here you are.

A: Your room number is 403. It's ④ **on the fourth** floor. ⑤ **Here is** your room key.

B: Thank you.

A: Breakfast will ⑥ **be served** from 7am to 9am on level B1. Please show your keycard to the staff.

B: OK.

A: ⑦ **If you have** any requests, please ⑧ **call** our front desk. Enjoy your stay.

中文翻譯請見 P. 92-93。

四、聽寫：請聽音檔，並將答案填入空格中。

A: Good afternoon. How may I help you today?

B: ① **I would like to check-in.**

A: Certainly. Do you have a reservation?

B: Yes, I do.

A: Could you please give me your name?

B: My name is Chen. ② **This is the confirmation slip.**

A: Ms. Chen… yes, we have your reservation. Please fill out this registration form.

B: OK.

A: May I have your credit card ③ **for a deposit?**

B: Sure. Here you are.

A: Your room number is 403. It's on the fourth floor. ④ **Here is your room key.**

B: Thank you.

A: Breakfast will be served from 7am to 9am ⑤ **on level B1**. Please show your keycard to the staff.

B: OK.

A: ⑥ **If you have any requests**, please call our front desk. Enjoy your stay.

中文翻譯請見 P. 92-93。

Calling the Front Desk
打電話給櫃檯人員

mp3-19

Dialogue A: Filing a Complaint
(A: Front desk clerk / B: Guest)

A Hello. This is the front desk.

B Hi, I have a problem in my room.

A I see. How can I help you?

B The air conditioning doesn't work. Could you send someone to fix it?

A I'm terribly sorry about that. What's your room number, please?

B 403.

A Okay, I'll send someone up in just a minute.

B Thank you.

Chinese Translation
中文翻譯

會話A：客房投訴
（A：櫃檯人員／B：房客）

A：您好，這裡是櫃檯。
B：你好，我的房間有個問題。
A：好的，我可以如何幫助您呢？
B：空調不會運轉，能請你派人來修理它嗎？
A：我對此感到非常抱歉。請問您的房號是多少？
B：403。
A：好的。我馬上派人上去。
B：謝謝你。

Dialogue B: Asking for Replacements
(A: Front desk clerk / B: Guest)

A Reception, may I help you?

B Yes. The towels in my room are dirty. Can I please have them changed?

A I apologize for that. I will send someone from housekeeping up with replacements right away. Is there anything else that you need?

B Yes. I can't have access to the Internet.

A Did you already try the password to log in?

B Yes, I did. But it still doesn't connect to the Internet.

A I see. I will send the IT person up to you shortly.

B Great, thanks.

Chinese Translation
中文翻譯

會話B：要求提供替換品
（A：櫃檯人員 / B：房客）

A：這裡是櫃檯。我可以為您服務嗎？

B：是的，我房間裡的毛巾很髒。能幫我換新的嗎？

A：我為此感到很抱歉。我會立即派客房部人員帶替換品上去。您還有其他需求嗎？

B：有的，我無法使用網路。

A：您已經嘗試過用密碼登錄了嗎？

B：是的，我那麼做了，但是它仍然沒有連接到網路。

A：了解。我會盡快派技術人員過去為您處理。

B：太好了，謝謝。

Vocabulary 生詞

❶ access (n.) （電腦）存取；使用

❷ air conditioning (n.) 空調

❸ housekeeping (n.) 客房部門

❹ minute (n.) 分鐘；一會兒、片刻

❺ reception (n.) 接待櫃檯

❻ replacement (n.) 替換品

❼ towel (n.) 毛巾

❽ apologize (v.) 道歉

⑨ complain (v.) 投訴；抱怨

⑩ connect (v.) 連接

⑪ fix (v.) 修理

⑫ log in 登入

⑬ work (v.) 工作；（機器等）運轉、活動

⑭ dirty (adj.) 骯髒的

⑮ shortly (adv.) 立刻、馬上

⑯ terribly (adv.) 非常地

Room Amenities 房間設施

lamp
燈、桌燈

sofa
沙發

minibar
（飯店客房內的）
小冰箱、酒櫃

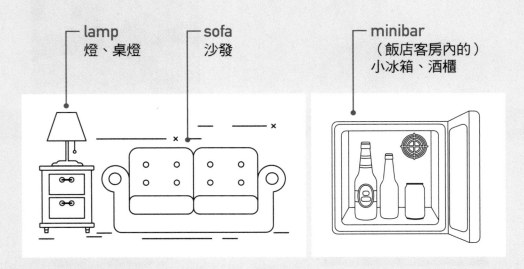

shampoo
洗髮乳

bathtub
浴缸

sink
洗臉槽

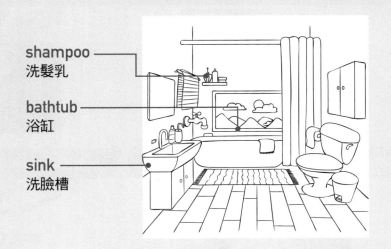

1

需要向飯店投訴時，你可以說：

1 **We have a problem in our room.** 我們的房間有問題。

2 **There seems to be a problem with 名詞.** ……似乎有問題。

例：**There seems to be a problem with the bathroom.** 浴室似乎有問題。

3 **There is something wrong with 名詞.** ……有問題。

例：**There is something wrong with the Internet connection.** 網路連線有問題。

4 **I'm not satisfied with the service I am receiving.** 我對我得到的服務並不滿意。

2

有東西損壞時，你可以說：

1 **名詞 is broken.** ……壞了。

例：**The hair dryer is broken.** 吹風機壞了。

2 **名詞 is out of order.** ……發生故障。

例：**The refrigerator is out of order.** 冰箱發生故障。

3 **名詞 doesn't work.** ……不能使用。

例：**The electric kettle doesn't work.** 電熱水壺不能使用。

4 **名詞 is not working.** ……不能運轉。

例：**The air conditioner is not working.** 冷氣機不能運轉。

3 住飯店時常遇到的問題：

1 **The toilet won't flush.** 馬桶不能沖水。

2 **I can't turn on the TV.** 電視打不開。

3 **I've lost my keycard.** 我弄丟鑰匙卡了。

4 **I'm out of toilet paper.** 我沒有衛生紙了。

5 **I can't connect to the Internet.** 我無法連接到網路。

6 **There is no hot water in the shower.** 淋浴間沒有熱水。

7 **This room smells.** 這個房間有臭味。

8 **I can't open the safe in my room.** 我無法打開房間的保險箱。

9 **The window in my room won't open.** 我房間裡的窗戶打不開。

10 **One of the lights won't come on.** 其中一個燈不亮。

11 **I've spilled coffee on the floor.** 我把咖啡灑在地板上了。

12 **I've locked myself out.** 我把自己鎖在門外了。

13 **The room next door is very noisy.
   I can't sleep.** 隔壁房間的人很吵。我睡不著。

14 **I ordered room service 30 minutes
   ago, but it has not arrived yet.** 我 30 分鐘前訂了客房服務，但現在還沒有到。

4 想要求飯店處理問題時，你可以說：

1 **Could you please come and check what's happening?**　　能請你來看看發生了什麼事嗎？

2 **Is it possible to change to another room?**　　是否可以更換房間？

3 **Could someone please come by to have a look?**　　有人可以過來看看嗎？

4 **Would it be possible to have a new one brought up?**　　可以送一個新的上來給我嗎？

5 常用的道歉說法：

1 **I am terribly sorry about ...**　　我對於……感到非常抱歉。

2 **I apologize for ...**　　我為……道歉。

Grammar 文法

01 Send 人 (to) 場所 派某人至某場所
Send 人 to 人 派某人至另一人的所在之處

例 Would you please send someone to my room to have a look? | 能請你派人到我房間看看嗎？

I will send someone up to you with a replacement. | 我會派人帶替換品過去給您。

02 Can I please 動詞 ? 我能……？

例 Can I please extend my stay till the day after tomorrow? | 能將我的住宿延長至後天嗎？

Can I please call you back later? | 可以待會回電給你嗎？

03 have（使役動詞）＋目的語＋動詞（過去分詞）

例 I had my hair cut yesterday. | 我昨天（有請人幫我）剪頭髮。

I must have my computer fixed. | 我必須（找人）把我的電腦修好。

I had my wallet stolen. | 我的錢包被偷了。

04 in just a minute （一下子）/ shortly （很快）
right away （馬上）/ immediately （立即）

例 I will come in just a minute. | 我一下子就到。

I will send someone to you shortly. | 我很快就會派人過去。

Exercise 練習

一、生詞填空：請將適當的生詞填入空格中。

> connect / terribly / fixed / replacement / log in /
> shortly / apologize / air conditioning

1. I can't _____ my computer to the Internet.

2. A new _____ costs at least $20,000.

3. I forgot my password and couldn't _____ .

4. He asked for a _____ for the broken part.

5. I _____ for the late reply.

6. Bus will be arriving _____ .

7. I am going to have my car _____ tomorrow.

8. He is _____ tired.

二、問答：請用英語回答下列問題。

1. 當你想表達電熱水壺壞了時，可以怎麼說？

_____

2. 當你想表達淋浴間沒有熱水時，可以怎麼說？

_____

3. 當你要抱怨房間浴室有問題時，該怎麼說？

_____

4. 當你要求派人來房間檢查情況（問題）時，你可以怎麼說？

_____

三、文法填空：請將適當的句型填入空格中。

> Did you already / in just a minute / doesn't work / with / up to
> send / Is there anything else / I'm terribly

A: Hello. This is the front desk.

B: Hi, I have a problem in my room.

A: I see. How can I help you?

B: The air conditioning ① _____ . Could you send someone to fix it?

A: ② _____ sorry about that. What's your room number, please?

B: 403.

A: Okay, I'll send someone up ③ _____ .

B: Thank you.

A: Reception, may I help you?

B: Yes. The towels in my room are dirty. Can I please have them changed?

A: I apologize for that. I will send someone from housekeeping up ④ _____
   replacements right away. ⑤ _____ that you need?

B: Yes. I can't have access to the Internet.

A: ⑥ _____ try the password to log in?

B: Yes, I did. But it still doesn't connect to the Internet.

A: I see. I will ⑦ _____ the IT person ⑧ _____ you shortly.

B: Great, thanks.

四、聽寫：請聽音檔，並將答案填入空格中。　　　　mp3-21

A: Hello. This is the front desk.

B: Hi. ① _____

A: I'm terribly sorry about that. How can I help you?

B: ② _____

A: I see. I'll send someone up in just a minute.

_____

A: Reception, may I help you?

B: The cups in my room are dirty. Can I please ③ _____

A: ④ _____ I will send someone up

with replacements right away. Is there anything else that you need?

B: Yes. ⑤ _____

A: Did you already try the password to log in?

B: Yes, I did. ⑥ _____

A: OK. I will send the IT person up to you shortly.

B: Great, thanks.

第七課 練習解答‧中文翻譯

一、生詞填空：請將適當的生詞填入空格中。

1. I can't **connect** my computer to the Internet.
   我沒辦法使電腦連接上網路。

2. A new **air conditioning** costs at least $20,000.
   新空調的價格至少要 20,000 元。

3. I forgot my password and couldn't **log in**.
   我忘記密碼了，無法登入。

4. He asked for a **replacement** for the broken part.
   他要求要一個替換品，以替換損壞的零件。

5. I **apologize** for the late reply.
   我為遲來的答覆道歉。

6. Bus will be arriving **shortly**.
   公車將很快到達。

7. I am going to have my car **fixed** tomorrow.
   我明天要（請人）修理我的車。

8. He is **terribly** tired.
   他非常地疲倦。

二、問答：請用英語回答下列問題。

1. **The electric kettle doesn't work.**　　電熱水壺不能使用。

2. **There is no hot water in the shower.**　　淋浴間沒有熱水。

3. **There seems to be a problem with the bathroom.**　　浴室似乎有問題。

4. **Could you please come and check what's happening?**　　能請你來看看發生了什麼事嗎？

三、文法填空：請將適當的句型填入空格中。

A: Hello. This is the front desk.

B: Hi, I have a problem in my room.

A: I see. How can I help you?

B: The air conditioning ① **doesn't work**. Could you send someone to fix it?

A: ② **I'm terribly** sorry about that. What's your room number, please?

B: 403.

A: Okay, I'll send someone up ③ **in just a minute**.

B: Thank you.

A: Reception, may I help you?

B: Yes. The towels in my room are dirty. Can I please have them changed?

A: I apologize for that. I will send someone from housekeeping up ④ **with** replacements right away. ⑤ **Is there anything else** that you need?

B: Yes. I can't have access to the Internet.

A: ⑥ **Did you already** try the password to log in?

B: Yes, I did. But it still doesn't connect to the Internet.

A: I see. I will ⑦ **send** the IT person ⑧ **up to** you shortly.

B: Great, thanks.

中文翻譯請見 P. 109,111。

四、聽寫：請聽音檔，並將答案填入空格中。

A: Hello. This is the front desk.

B: Hi. ① **There seems to be a problem with the bathroom.**

A: I'm terribly sorry about that. How can I help you?

B: ② **The toilet won't flush.**

A: I see. I'll send someone up in just a minute.

A: Reception, may I help you?

B: The cups in my room are dirty. Can I please ③ **have them changed?**

A: ④ **I am terribly sorry.** I will send someone up with replacements right away. Is there anything else that you need?

B: Yes. ⑤ **I can't connect to the Internet.**

A: Did you already try the password to log in?

B: Yes, I did. ⑥ **But it still doesn't connect to the Internet.**

A: OK. I will send the IT person up to you shortly.

B: Great, thanks.

中文翻譯

A：您好，這裡是櫃檯。
B：你好。浴室似乎有問題。
A：我感到非常抱歉。我可以如何幫助您呢？
B：廁所不能沖水。
A：了解。我會馬上派人過去。

A：這裡是櫃檯。我可以為您服務嗎？
B：是的。我房間裡的杯子很髒。能請你更換它們嗎？

Ａ：我非常抱歉。我會立即要客房部的人帶替換品過去。您還有其他需求嗎？

Ｂ：有的。我無法使用網路。

Ａ：您已經嘗試過用密碼登入了嗎？

Ｂ：是的，我那麼做了。但是它仍然沒有連接到網路。

Ａ：好的。我會盡快派技術人員為您處理。

Ｂ：太好了，謝謝。

Checking-out at the Hotel
在飯店辦理退房手續

mp3-22

 Dialogue 會話

Dialogue A: I am Checking-out.
(A: Guest / B: Front desk clerk)

A Hi, I am checking-out. Here is the key.

B Certainly. Ms. Hui-ling Zhan?

A Yes, I am.

B Thank you very much. Just a moment, please. (*prints out a receipt*) Your bill comes to 265 dollars.

A I think there is a mistake in the calculation of my bill. What is this charge for? (*points to an item on the statement*)

B Did you take anything from the minibar?

A Oh, yes. I forgot I had a beer and a mineral water.

B That is all right. How would you like to pay?

A I'd like to pay by cash.

Chinese Translation
中文翻譯

會話A：請幫我辦理退房。
（A：房客／B：櫃檯人員）

A：嗨，請幫我辦理退房。這是鑰匙。

B：沒問題。是詹慧玲女士嗎？

A：是的，我是。

B：非常感謝。請稍等一下。（印出一份帳單）您的帳單共計 265 美元。

A：我認為我的帳單計算有錯誤。這個是為什麼收費呢？（指出帳單上的一個項目）

B：您有從小冰箱拿取任何東西嗎？

A：喔，是的。我忘記我喝了一罐啤酒和一瓶礦泉水。

B：沒關係。您想要如何付款呢？

A：我想用現金付款。

Dialogue B: Could You Please Call Me a Taxi?

(A: Guest / B: Front desk clerk)

A Could you please call me a taxi?

B Sure. Where to?

A To the Second Airport's International Terminal.

B Certainly. (*makes a phone call*)

B The taxi will be here within 5 minutes, outside the entrance. I hope you enjoyed your stay and have a good journey.

A Yes, I enjoyed my stay. Thank you very much.

Chinese Translation
中文翻譯

會話B：可以幫我打電話叫計程車嗎？
（A：房客 / B：櫃檯人員）

A：可以幫我打電話叫計程車嗎？

B：好的。去哪裡？

A：到第二機場的國際航廈。

B：沒問題。（撥打電話）

B：計程車將在 5 分鐘內抵達飯店入口處。我希望您對這次的住宿還滿意，並
　 祝福您旅途愉快。

A：是的，我很滿意。非常感謝你。

1 check out (v.) 辦理退房

2 bill (n.) 帳單；帳款

3 moment (n.) 片刻

4 calculation (n.) 計算

5 charge (n.) 費用

6 mineral water (n.) 礦泉水

7 pay (v.) 支付

8 cash (v.) 現金

9 terminal (n.) 航廈

International Terminal 國際航廈
Domestic Terminal 國內航廈

10 stay (n.) 住宿

11 journey (n.) 旅程

12 shuttle service 接駁車服務

1

想要延後退房時，你可以說：

1 I'd like to stay in the room until 2pm. Is that OK?
我想留在房間直到下午 2 點。可以嗎？

2 Can I stay in my room until 6pm?
我可以留在我的房間直到下午 6 點嗎？

2

結帳時，若對發票內容有疑問，你可以說：

1 What is this charge for?
這個是收取什麼費用呢？

2 What is this amount for?
這個金額是做什麼用的？

3 I didn't use any pay channel.
我沒有使用任何付費頻道。

4 I took nothing from the minibar.
我沒有從小冰箱裡拿東西。

5 I think this amount for "room service fee" is not correct.
我認為「客房服務費」的金額不正確。

6 May I please have an itemized bill?
我可以有個列出項目的帳單嗎？

3

需要行李服務時，你可以說：

1 Could you please help me with my luggage?
你能幫我拿我的行李嗎？

2 Would it be OK if I leave my baggage here?
如果我把行李留在這裡，可以嗎？

3 Would you mind if I leave my luggage here at the reception till this afternoon?
你介意我把行李寄放在櫃台直到今天下午嗎？

4　需要交通服務時，你可以說：

1 **Would you call me a taxi, please?**　　請你幫我叫一輛計程車好嗎？

2 **Do you have shuttle service to the airport?**　　你們有提供機場接駁服務嗎？

3 **Could you call us a taxi for the airport, please?**　　可以幫我們叫一輛計程車到機場嗎？

5　退房時，想對服務人員表達感謝，你可以說：

1 **I had a great stay. I would love to come again.**　　我住得很愉快。還會想再來。

2 **We love this hotel very much. I will certainly come back again. Thank you for everything.**　　我們非常喜歡這家飯店。我一定會再回來的。謝謝你所做的一切。

Grammar 文法

01 come to (=reach) 達到；共計

例 Water comes to the boiling point at 100 degrees Celsius.　水在攝氏 100 度達到沸點。

How much does it come to?　共計多少錢？

02 charge for 收費

例 How much do you charge for this service?　這個服務你收費多少錢？

The museum charges for admission.　博物館收取入場費。

03 pay by cash / credit card / check (cheque) / direct deposit

以現金／信用卡／支票／存款帳戶支付

例 A: Can I pay by credit card?　可以以信用卡支付嗎？

B: We do not accept credit cards. Please pay by cash.　我們不接受信用卡。請用現金支付。

> 小提醒：「by」= 方法

例 travel by car / bus / train / plane / bike　用開車／搭巴士／搭火車／搭飛機／騎自行車的方式去旅遊

contact me by phone / email / fax　用打電話／寫電子郵件／發傳真的方式聯絡我

04 Where to? (=Where would you like to go?) （口語）去哪裡？

例 Taxi driver: Where to?　計程車司機：去哪裡？

You: Gloria Hotel, please.　你：葛洛莉旅館，謝謝。

05 **within** 某範圍「以內」～

例 You must finish this paper within a week.　你必須在本週內完成這份報告。

I will be back within 30 minutes.　我會在 30 分內回來。

> 小提醒：in 在……期間內；在……期間之後
> within 在一定時間內

06 **I hope ＋現在簡單式／未來簡單式**

例 I hope you have a good day.　我希望你有美好的一天。

I hope it will stop raining tomorrow.　我希望明天會停止下雨。

Exercise 練習

一、生詞填空：請將適當的生詞填入空格中。

> journey / shuttle / bill / mineral water
> calculation / terminal / check out / cash

1. If you are out of ＿＿＿＿＿＿＿＿＿＿＿, you can pay by credit card.

2. Can I have 2 bottles of ＿＿＿＿＿＿＿＿＿＿, please?

3. If you want to ＿＿＿＿＿＿＿＿＿ later than 10am, please inform reception before 9am.

4. My flight departs from ＿＿＿＿＿＿＿＿＿ 2.

5. Do you have ＿＿＿＿＿＿＿ service to the airport?

6. I will pay the ＿＿＿＿＿＿＿.

7. I hope you have a pleasant ＿＿＿＿＿＿＿＿.

8. There's some error in the ＿＿＿＿＿＿＿＿.

二、問答：請用英語回答下列問題。

1. 如何詢問是否可以將退房時間延長至下午 3 點？

＿＿＿＿＿＿＿＿＿＿＿＿＿＿＿＿＿＿＿＿＿＿＿＿＿＿＿

2. 付錢時，你認為住宿費有些問題，該怎麼說？

＿＿＿＿＿＿＿＿＿＿＿＿＿＿＿＿＿＿＿＿＿＿＿＿＿＿＿

3. 想將行李寄存在櫃台時，該如何說？

＿＿＿＿＿＿＿＿＿＿＿＿＿＿＿＿＿＿＿＿＿＿＿＿＿＿＿

4. 想請人幫忙叫一輛計程車去機場，該如何說？

＿＿＿＿＿＿＿＿＿＿＿＿＿＿＿＿＿＿＿＿＿＿＿＿＿＿＿

三、文法填空：請將適當的句型填入空格中。

> within / Could you please / charge for / I hope / comes to
> by / Where to

A: Hi, I am checking out. Here is the key.

B: Certainly. Ms. Hui-ling Zhan?

A: Yes, I am.

B: Thank you very much. Just a moment please. (*prints out a receipt*) Your bill

   ① _____ 265 dollars.

A: I think there is a mistake in the calculation of my bill. What is this

   ② _____ ? (*points to an item on the statement*)

B: Did you take anything from the minibar?

A: Oh, yes. I forgot I had a beer and a mineral water.

B: That is all right. How would you like to pay?

A: I'd like to pay ③ _____ cash.

A: ④ _____ call me a taxi?

B: Sure. ⑤ _____ ?

A: To the Second Airport's International Terminal.

B: Certainly. (*makes a phone call*)

B: The taxi will be here ⑥ _____ 5 minutes, outside the entrance.

   ⑦ _____ you enjoyed your stay and have a good journey.

A: Yes, I enjoyed my stay. Thank you very much.

四、聽寫：請聽音檔，並將答案填入空格中。　　　　　　　　　mp3-24

A: ① _____. Here is the key.

B: Certainly. Ms. Hui-ling Zhan?

A: Yes, I am.

B: Thank you very much. Just a moment please. (*prints out a receipt*) Your bill comes to 265 dollars.

A: There must be some mistake.

　② _____ (*points to an item on the statement*)

B: Did you take anything from the minibar?

A: Oh, yes. I had one beer. Sorry I forgot about that!

B: That is all right. How would you like to pay?

A: ③ _____

_____

A: ④ _____

B: Sure. Where to?

A: To the Second Airport's International Terminal.

B: Certainly. (*makes a phone call*)

B: ⑤ _____, outside the entrance.

　We hope to see you back here soon.

A: Yes, ⑥ _____. Thank you very much.

第八課 練習解答‧中文翻譯

一、生詞填空：請將適當的生詞填入空格中。

1. If you are out of **cash**, you can pay by credit card.
   如果你沒有現金，你可以用信用卡付款。

2. Can I have 2 bottles of **mineral water**, please?
   請問我可以要兩瓶礦泉水嗎？

3. If you want to **check out** later than 10am, please inform reception before 9am.
   如果你想在上午 10 點以後退房，請在上午 9 點前通知櫃台。

4. My flight departs from **terminal** 2.
   我的航班從第 2 航廈出發。

5. Do you have **shuttle** service to the airport?
   你們有到機場的接駁服務嗎？

6. I will pay the **bill**.
   我要付帳。

7. I hope you have a pleasant **journey**.
   我希望您有一個愉快的旅程。

8. There's some error in the **calculation**.
   計算有點錯誤。

二、問答：請用英語回答下列問題。

1. **I'd like to stay in the room until 3pm. Is that OK?**

   我想留在房間後到下午 3 點。可以嗎？

2. **I think there is a mistake in the calculation of my bill.**

   我認為我的帳單計算有錯誤。

3. **Would you mind if I leave my luggage here at the reception?**

   你介意我把行李寄放在櫃檯嗎？

4. **Could you call us a taxi for the airport, please?**

   可以幫我們叫一輛計程車去機場嗎？

三、文法填空：請將適當的句型填入空格中。

A: Hi, I am checking out. Here is the key.

B: Certainly. Ms. Hui-ling Zhan?

A: Yes, I am.

B: Thank you very much. Just a moment please. (*prints out a receipt*) Your bill

   ① **comes to** 265 dollars.

A: I think there is a mistake in the calculation of my bill. What is this ② **charge for**?

   (*points to an item on the statement*)

B: Did you take anything from the minibar?

A: Oh, yes. I forgot I had a beer and a mineral water.

B: That is all right. How would you like to pay?

A: I'd like to pay ③ **by** cash.

A: ④ **Could you please** call me a taxi?

B: Sure. ⑤ **Where to**?

A: To the Second Airport's International Terminal.

B: Certainly. (*makes a phone call*)

B: The taxi will be here ⑥ **within** 5 minutes, outside the entrance. ⑦ **I hope** you enjoyed your stay and have a good journey.

A: Yes, I enjoyed my stay. Thank you very much.

中文翻譯請見 P. 127,129。

四、聽寫：請聽音檔，並將答案填入空格中。

A: ① **Hi, I am checking out.** Here is the key.

B: Certainly. Ms. Hui-ling Zhan?

A: Yes, I am.

B: Thank you very much. Just a moment please. (*prints out a receipt*) Your bill comes to 265 dollars.

A: There must be some mistake. ② **What is this charge for?** (*points to an item on the statement*)

B: Did you take anything from the minibar?

A: Oh, yes. I had one beer. Sorry I forgot about that!

B: That is all right. How would you like to pay?

A: ③ **By cash, please.**

A: ④ **Would you call me a taxi, please?**

B: Sure. Where to?

A: To the Second Airport's International Terminal.

B: Certainly. (*makes a phone call*)

B: ⑤ **The taxi will be here in a few minutes,** outside the entrance.

　　We hope to see you back here soon.

B: Yes, ⑥ **I would love to come back again.** Thank you very much.

中文翻譯

A：請幫我辦理退房。這是鑰匙。

B：沒問題。詹慧玲女士？

A：是的，我是。

B：非常感謝。請稍等。（印出一份帳單）您的帳單共計 265 美元。

A：我認為我的帳單計算有錯誤。這個是什麼收費呢？（指出帳單上的一個項目）

B：您有從小冰箱拿取任何東西嗎？

A：喔，是的。我喝了一罐啤酒。對不起我忘記了！

B：沒關係。您想要如何付款？

A：用現金，謝謝。

A：可以幫我叫一輛計程車嗎？

B：好的。去哪裡？

A：到第二機場的國際航廈。

B：沒問題。（撥打電話）

B：計程車將在幾分鐘內到達入口門外。我們希望很快就會再見到您。

A：是的，我很樂意再次光臨。非常感謝你。

Taking a Taxi
搭計程車

mp3-25

Dialogue 會話

Dialogue A: Could We Stop by the Nearest Bank?
(A: Driver / B: Passenger)

A Good morning. How are you?

B I'm good, thank you. I have two suitcases. Would you mind opening the trunk for me?

A Certainly.

(*Passenger puts suitcases in the trunk and gets in the taxi*)

A Where to?

B To ABC Hotel, please. Here's the address. How much to get there?

A It'll be about 50 dollars.

B I'm sorry... I don't have enough money. Would it be possible for us to stop by the nearest bank first? I apologize for the inconvenience!

A No problem, ma'am. Please fasten your seat belt.

B OK. Thank you!

Chinese Translation
中文翻譯

會話A：能在最近的銀行暫停一下嗎？
（A：司機／B：乘客）

A：早安。您好嗎？

B：我很好，謝謝。我有兩個行李箱。你介意幫我打開後車廂嗎？

A：沒問題。

（乘客將行李箱放入後車廂，並坐進計程車內）

A：去哪裡呢？

B：請到 ABC 飯店。地址在這裡。到那裡要多少錢？

A：大約要 50 元。

B：抱歉……我沒有足夠的錢。我們有沒有可能先去最近的銀行暫停一下呢？
造成不便，我很抱歉！

A：沒問題，夫人。請繫上您的安全帶。

B：好的。謝謝你！

Dialogue B: How Much Longer Will It Take?
(A: Driver / B: Passenger)

B How much longer will it take?

A It takes another 10 minutes.

B I see. I am kind of in a hurry. I've got to be there by 10am...

A OK, I will drive a little faster.

(*Taxi pulls up in front of destination*)

A Here we are. It's 55 dollars, please.

B Here's 60 dollars. Please keep the change.

A Thanks a lot! Here's your receipt. Have a nice day!

Chinese Translation
中文翻譯

會話B：還需要多久才會到呢？
（A：司機 / B：乘客）

B：還需要多久才會到呢？
A：還要再 10 分鐘。
B：我明白了。我有點趕時間。我必須在上午 10 點前到那裡……
A：好的。我會開快一點。

（計程車在目的地前停下來）
A：我們到了。總共是 55 元，謝謝您。
B：這裡有 60 元。請不用找零。
A：非常感謝！這是您的收據。祝您有美好的一天！

mp3-26

1 suitcase (n.) 行李箱

2 trunk (n.) 後車廂

3 ma'am (n.) 夫人；女士

4 fasten (v.) 繫上

5 seat belt (n.) 安全帶

6 take (v.) 拿取；花（時間）

7 a little 有點；少許

8 hurry (n. / v.) 匆忙；趕緊

❾ keep (v.) 保留

Useful Expressions
實用短句

1 告知司機要去哪裡時，你可以說：

1 **Can you take me to the ABC Hotel, please?**　能請你帶我到 ABC 飯店嗎？

2 **I have 2 destinations. First, go to A, then go to B, please.**　我有兩個目的地。請先去 A，再去 B。

2 當有大件行李時，你可以說：

1 **I have two suitcases. Could you put them in the trunk?**　我有兩個行李箱。你可以把它們放在後車廂嗎？

2 **Can you open the trunk for me?**　你可以幫我打開後車廂嗎？

3 想詢問車程所需時間，你可以說：

1 **How long does it take to get there?**　到那裡需要花多少時間？

2 **Do you know how long it might take?**　你知道可能要花多少時間嗎？

4 想詢問車資時，你可以說：

1 **How much will it be?**　多少錢？

2 **How much will it cost?**　要花多少錢？

3 **Are there any other extra charges?**　還有其他額外費用嗎？

4 **Can you take me there for 50 dollars?**　付 50 元的話，你能帶我去那裡嗎？

5 **Could you turn on the meter, please?**　可以請你按下跳表嗎？

5 當你趕時間時，你可以說：

1 **Can you get there by 10?**   你能 10 點前到那裡嗎？

2 **I am in a hurry. Could you hurry up a little bit?**   我很趕時間，你能趕快一點（開快一點）嗎？

3 **Take the shortest route, please.**   請走最短的路線。

6 當你想指路時，可以說：

1 **Can you make a right / left turn?**   你能右／左轉嗎？

2 **Keep on going straight.**   繼續直行。

3 **Go in the driveway.**   進入車道。

4 **Stop in front of the ABC Theater.**   在 ABC 劇院前停下來。

5 **Can you take the 3rd Avenue instead of the 5th?**   你能走第三大道而不是第五大道嗎？

6 **Could you take this route to the Central Terminal?**   你能走這條路線到中央航站嗎？

7 當你想在中途下車時，可以說：

1 **Please drop me off here.**   請讓我在這裡下車。

2 **I will get off here, thank you.**   我要在這裡下車，謝謝你。

3 **Here is fine.**   這裡就好。

4 **Could you pull over here?**   能在這裡停車嗎？

8 付費時，你可以說：

1 May I have a receipt, please? 　　　我可以要收據嗎？謝謝。

2 You can keep the change, thanks. 　　不用找零，謝謝。

9 在計程車上與司機輕鬆小聊：

1 A: Where are you from? 　　　　　　你來自哪裡？

　 B: I'm from Taiwan. 　　　　　　　我來自台灣。

2 A: What brings you to Brisbane? 　　你是為了什麼而來到布里斯本呢？

　 B: I'm here on vacation. 　　　　　我來這裡是為了渡假。

3 A: How was your flight? 　　　　　　你的航程如何？

　 B: It was okay, though my flight was 　還好，儘管我的航班延誤了一個
　　　delayed for an hour. 　　　　　　小時。

4 A: How long are you staying? 　　　　你會待多久時間？

　 B: For 5 days. 　　　　　　　　　　五天。

5 A: Is this your first time in Boston? 　這是你第一次來波士頓嗎？

　 B: Yes, it is. 　　　　　　　　　　是的。

6 A: Are you enjoying New York? 　　　你在紐約玩得開心嗎？

　 B: Yes, very much. 　　　　　　　　是的，非常開心。

01 How much to 場所 ? (=How much does it cost to 場所 ?)

到某場所需要花費多少錢

例 How much to Brisbane Airport? 到布里斯本機場要多少錢？

How much to ABC Zoo? 到 ABC 動物園要多少錢？

02 It takes 時間　花費多少時間

例 It takes another hour. 需要再花一小時。

How long does it take to finish your work? 完成你的工作需要花多久時間？

03 stop by　（通常是順路的狀況）短暫停留

例 I stopped by a convenience store for some bread. 為了買些麵包，我在便利商店暫停一下。

Why don't you stop by for a little while? 你為何不順路過來停留一會兒？

04 how much longer　還要再多久的時間

例 About how much longer should I wait? 我還要再等待多久的時間？

How much longer will it take for the food to arrive? 還要再多久時間食物才會送達？

05 **Would you mind 動詞 ing 型 ...?** 你介意⋯⋯嗎？

(比「Do you mind 動詞 ing 型 ?」更加禮貌的說法)

例 Would you mind opening the window?　　　　　你介意打開窗戶嗎？

Would you mind bringing me a glass of water?　你介意帶杯水給我嗎？

回答時請注意：

否定：No, I don't. / All right. / OK. / No problem. / Sure.

　　　不，我不介意。請那麼做吧，沒關係。

肯定：Yes, I do. / I'm sorry but...

　　　是，我介意。很抱歉，但⋯⋯

---

06 **Got to 動詞原型 . (= I have got to 動詞原型 .)** 必須、非得做某件事不可了。

例 I've got to go.　　　　　　　　　　　　　　我必須要離開了。

I've got to hurry up.　　　　　　　　　　　我得加快速度了。

07 **by 時間** 在⋯⋯之前

例 Please come here by 6.　　　　　　　　　　請六點前來這裡。

I will be there by 3.　　　　　　　　　　　我會三點前到那裡。

08 **kind of** 有點

例 I am kind of hungry.　　　　　　　　　　　我有點餓。

The movie was kind of boring.　　　　　　　這電影有點無聊。

Exercise 練習

一、生詞填空：請將適當的生詞填入空格中。

> Hurry / ma'am / longer / suitcase / take
> fasten / trunk / kind of

1. Could I keep my _____ at the hotel until 3pm?

2. Please _____ your seat belt.

3. May I help you, _____?

4. My car _____ is full of baggage.

5. It does not _____ much time to finish this work.

6. _____ up! Or we will miss our flight.

7. A: Would you like some more tea?

   B: No thanks. I am _____ full.

8. How much _____ does it take to get there?

二、問答：請用英語回答下列問題。

1. 如何請司機帶你去 ABC 機場？

_____

2. 當想把行李放在後車廂裡時，該說什麼？

_____

3. 如何請司機按下跳表？

_____

4. 當趕時間時，該如何說？

_____

5. 當想在中途下車，該怎麼說？

_____

三、文法填空：請將適當的句型填入空格中。

> **Would you mind / kind of / keep the change / How much to**
> **Here we are / by / stop by / It takes / got to**

A: Good morning. How are you?

B: I'm good, thank you. I have two suitcases. ① _____ opening the trunk for me?

A: Certainly.

(*Passenger puts suitcases in the trunk and gets in the taxi*)

A: Where to?

B: To ABC Hotel, please. Here's the address. ② _____ get there?

A: It'll be about 50 dollars.

B: I'm sorry... I don't have enough money. Would it be possible for us to

③ _____ the nearest bank first? I apologize for the inconvenience!

A: No problem, ma'am. Please fasten your seat belt.

B: OK. Thank you!

_____

B: How much longer will it take?

A: ④ _____ another 10 minutes.

B: I see. I am ⑤ _____ in a hurry. I've ⑥ _____ be there

⑦ _____ 10.

A: OK, I will drive a little faster.

_____

(*Taxi pulls up in front of destination*)

A: ⑧ _____ . It's 55 dollars, please.

B: Here's 60 dollars. Please ⑨ _____ .

A: Thanks a lot! Here's your receipt. Have a nice day!

四、聽寫：請聽音檔，並將答案填入空格中。 mp3-27

A: Good morning. How are you?

B: ① _____ , thank you.

  I have two suitcases. Could you open the trunk for me?

A: Certainly.

(*Passenger puts suitcases in the trunk and gets in the taxi*)

A: Where to?

B: To ABC Museum, please. ② _____

A: It'll be about 50 dollars.

B: I'm sorry... ③ _____ .

  Could you stop by the nearest bank first?

A: Yes, ma'am. Please fasten your seat belt.

B: OK. Thank you!

_____

B: ④ _____

A:　It takes another 10 minutes.

B: I see. ⑤ _____ Could you hurry up a little bit?

A: OK, I will try.

B: ⑥ _____

A: Certainly. It's 55 dollars, please.

B: Here's 60 dollars. Please keep the change.

A: Thank you very much. Have a nice day!

第九課 練習解答 · 中文翻譯

一、生詞填空：請將適當的生詞填入空格中。

1. Could I keep my **suitcase** at the hotel until 3pm?
   我可以將行李箱留在飯店直到下午 3 點嗎？

2. Please **fasten** your seat belt.
   請繫緊您的安全帶。

3. May I help you, **ma'am**?
   夫人我可以幫您嗎？

4. My car **trunk** is full of baggage.
   我的後車廂裝滿了行李。

5. It does not **take** much time to finish this work.
   完成這項工作不需要花很多時間。

6. **Hurry** up! Or we will miss our flight.
   加快腳步！不然我們會錯過航班。

7. A: Would you like some more tea?
      您還想要些茶嗎？

   B: No thanks. I am **kind of** full.
      不，謝謝。我有點飽了。

8. How much **longer** does it take to get there?
   到達那裡還需要多久的時間？

二、問答：請用英語回答下列問題。

1. **Could you take me to ABC Airport, please?**

   能請你帶我到 ABC 機場嗎？

2. **Could you put this baggage in the trunk?**

   能請你把這個行李放在後車廂嗎？

3. **Could you turn on the meter, please?**

   能請你按下跳表嗎？

4. **Could you hurry up a little bit?**

   你能趕快一點嗎？

5. **Please drop me off here.**

   請讓我在這裡下車。

三、文法填空：請將適當的句型填入空格中。

A: Good morning. How are you?

B: I'm good, thank you. I have two suitcases. ① **Would you mind** opening the trunk for me?

A: Certainly.

(*Passenger puts suitcases in the trunk and gets in the taxi*)

A: Where to?

B: To ABC Hotel, please. Here's the address. ② **How much to** get there?

A: It'll be about 50 dollars.

B: I'm sorry...I don't have enough money. Would it be possible for us to ③ **stop by** the nearest bank first? I apologize for the inconvenience!

A: No problem, ma'am. Please fasten your seat belt.

B: OK. Thank you!

B: How much longer will it take?

A: ④ **It takes** another 10 minutes.

B: I see. I am ⑤ **kind of** in a hurry. I've ⑥ **got to** be there ⑦ **by** 10.

A: OK, I will drive a little faster.

(*Taxi pulls up in front of destination*)

A: ⑧ **Here we are.** It's 55 dollars, please.

B: Here's 60 dollars. Please ⑨ **keep the change.**

A: Thanks a lot! Here's your receipt. Have a nice day!

中文翻譯請見 P. 145,147。

四、聽寫：請聽音檔，並將答案填入空格中。

A: Good morning. How are you?

B: ① **I'm good**, thank you. I have two suitcases. Could you open the trunk for me?

A: Certainly.

(*Passenger puts suitcases in the trunk and gets in the taxi*)

A: Where to?

B: To ABC Museum, please. ② **How much to get there?**

A: It'll be about 50 dollars.

B: I'm sorry... ③ **I don't have enough money.** Could you stop by the nearest bank first?

A: Yes, ma'am. Please fasten your seat belt.

B: OK. Thank you!

B: ④ **How much longer will it take?**

A: It takes another 10 minutes.

B: I see. ⑤ **I am in a hurry.** Could you hurry up a little bit?

A: OK, I will try.

B: ⑥ **Please drop me off here.**

A: Certainly. It's 55 dollars, please.

B: Here's 60 dollars. Please keep the change.

A: Thank you very much. Have a nice day!

A：早安。你好嗎？

B：我很好，謝謝。我有兩個手提箱。你可以幫我打開後車廂嗎？

A：沒問題。

（乘客將行李箱放入後車廂，並坐進計程車內）

A：去哪裡？

B：到 ABC 博物館。到那裡要多少錢？

A：大約 50 元。

B：對不起……我沒有足夠的錢。你能在最近的銀行先停一下嗎？

A：好的，夫人。請繫上您的安全帶。

B：好的，謝謝你！

B：還需要多久時間才會到那裡？

A：還需要再 10 分鐘。

B：我明白了。我有點趕時間。你能快一點嗎？

A：好的。我會試試。

B：請讓我在這裡下車。

A：好的。總共是 55 元。

B：這裡是 60 元，請不用找零。

A：非常謝謝您。祝您有愉快的一天！

Dining at a Restaurant
在餐廳用餐

Lesson 10 | 第十課

mp3-28

Dialogue 會話

Dialogue A: Before Entering a Restaurant
(A: Waitress / B: Guest)

(*guests approach the waiter station*)

A Hello! Do you have a reservation?

B No. Can we get a table for two, please?

A Smoking or non-smoking?

B Non-smoking, please.

A OK. I'll show you to your table. Please follow me.

B Thank you.

(*guests take their seats and reach for the menu*)

B Excuse me. Do you have a menu in Chinese?

A Yes. I'll bring some over to you immediately.

Chinese Translation
中文翻譯

會話A：進餐廳之前
（A：女服務生 / B：客人）

（有一組客人向櫃檯走來）
A：哈囉！請問有訂位嗎？
B：沒有。能幫我們安排兩個人用餐嗎？
A：吸煙（區）還是禁煙（區）？
B：禁菸（區）。
A：好的。我來為您們帶位。請跟我來。
B：謝謝你。
（客人入座並拿起菜單）
B：不好意思，你們有中文菜單嗎？
A：有的。我會馬上帶一些過來給您。

Dialogue B: Ordering at a Restaurant
(A: Waitress / B: Guest 1 / C: Guest 2)

A Good evening, my name is Mary. I'll be your server for tonight. Are you ready to order now?

B (*points to the menu*) Yes. Can I have this steak and this salad?

A Sure. How would you like your steak?

B Medium, please.

A How about you, ma'am?

C I'd like to start off with a shrimp cocktail.

A And for your main course?

C Um… fish fillet, please.

A Would you like some wine with your meal?

B Yes. 2 glasses of red wine, please.

A OK. Can I get you anything else?

B That's all for now. Let us keep the menu for a while.

Chinese Translation
中文翻譯

會話B：在餐廳點餐
（A：女服務生 / B：客人 1 / C：客人 2）

A：晚安，我是瑪莉。今晚將由我擔任您們的服務生。您們準備好要點餐了嗎？

B：（指向菜單）是的。可以給我這份牛排和這個沙拉嗎？

A：好的。您的牛排想要幾分熟呢？

B：請做五分熟。

A：那，夫人您呢？

C：我想先從鮮蝦雞尾酒開始。

A：您的主菜呢？

C：嗯……請給我魚排。

A：您們用餐時想要配點酒嗎？

B：是的，請給我們兩杯紅酒。

A：好的。還有需要其他的嗎？

B：目前只要這些就好。讓我們保留一下菜單。

Vocabulary 生詞

mp3-29

❶ waiter / waitress (n.) 男服務生／女服務生

❷ immediately (v.) 即刻、馬上

❸ order (v. / n.) 點餐

❹ recommend (v.) 推薦

❺ salad (n.) 沙拉

Dishware 餐具

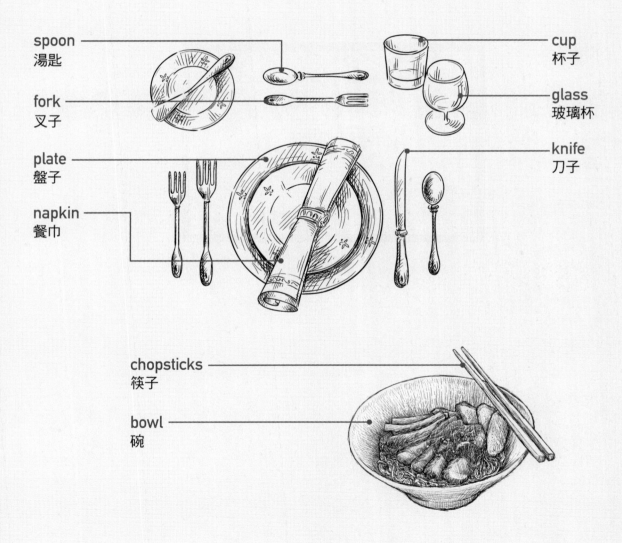

spoon
湯匙

fork
叉子

plate
盤子

napkin
餐巾

cup
杯子

glass
玻璃杯

knife
刀子

chopsticks
筷子

bowl
碗

Menu 菜單

Starters / Appetizers
開胃菜

Main courses
主菜

Soup
湯品

Desserts
甜點

Side dishes
小菜

Drinks / Beverages
飲料

Useful Expressions
實用短句

1 當服務員詢問用餐人數時，你可以回答：

1 **Just two.** 　　　　　　　　　　　只有兩人。

2 **We're 人數.** 　　　　　　　　　　我們幾人。

3 **It's only me.** 　　　　　　　　　　只有我一人。

2 當想要特定的座位時，你可以說：

1 **I'd like a private booth, please.** 　　請幫我安排一間私人包廂。

2 **Can I sit at that table?** 　　　　　　我能坐在那張桌子嗎？（通常搭配手勢，指向該桌）

3 **We are a large group. Is it possible to have us sit together?** 　　我們人數較多，有可能坐在一起嗎？

3 點餐的時候，你可以說：

1 **Can I have a menu? / Can we have some menu?** 　　我可以有菜單嗎？／我們可以有菜單嗎？

2 **Excuse me. We're ready to order, please.** 　　不好意思，我們可以點餐了。

3 **We will let you know when we have decided.** 　　我們決定後會讓你知道。

4 **What do you recommend?** 　　你有什麼推薦的嗎？

5 **Can I have 名詞?** 　　我可以有……？

6 **I'd like 名詞.** 　　我想要……。

7 I will have 名詞.   我要……。

8 I'd like the same one, please.   我想要一樣的，謝謝。

9 When do you take the last order?   最後點餐時間是幾點？

4 想詢問餐點的口味及烹調方式時，你可以說：

1 Is it sweet / spicy / sour / salty?   是甜的／辣的／酸的／鹹的嗎？

2 Is it steamed / fried / cooked / raw?   是蒸的／油炸的／熟的／生的嗎？

5 如何點牛排？

1 I'd like my steak rare / medium / well done, please.   我的牛排要一分熟／五分熟／全熟。

6 完成點餐時，你可以說：

1 That's all for now.   目前只要這些就好。

2 That's it for now.   目前只要這樣就好。

3 Let us keep the menu for a while.   讓我們保留一下菜單。

7 當想付款的時候，你可以說：

1 May I have the check / bill, please?   可以給我帳單嗎？（較有禮貌）

2 Check (Cheque) / Bill, please.   請結帳。

01 Table for 人數　幾人用餐

例　A table for 2, please.　　　　　　　　　　我們兩個人用餐。

　　Do you have a table for 3?　　　　　　　　你們有三個人用餐的位子嗎？

02 in 語言　用某種語言

例　She made a speech in English.　　　　　　她用英文發表演說。

　　I need to write a report in Japanese.　　　我需要用日文寫個報告。

03 start off with 名詞　由～開始

例　Let's start off with beer!　　　　　　　　讓我們從啤酒開始（這一餐）吧！

　　I'll start off with a cup of coffee, please.　我想先來一杯咖啡。

04 glass of 名詞　杯（單位）

例　My mother tells me to drink a glass of soy milk every day.　　我媽媽告訴我每天要喝一杯豆漿。

　　I drank a full glass of tomato juice.　　　我喝了一整杯番茄汁。

05 That's all for now.　目前只要這些就好。（常用於點餐時）

例　A: Anything else?　　　　　　　　　　　還有（需要）其他的嗎？

　　B: That's all for now.　　　　　　　　　目前只要這些就好。

> That's all for today.
> 今天就到這邊。（常用於課堂結束時，意思是「以上是今天全部的課程。」）

06 Let ＋人＋動詞原形　讓某人做某事

例　Dad, let us buy a new one!　　　　　　爸爸，讓我們買一個新的吧！

I'll let you know when I get home.　　我到家時會讓你知道（告訴你）。

一、生詞填空：請將適當的生詞填入空格中。

napkin / waitress / immediately / menu
recommend / order

1. Could you give me a clean _____ , please?

2. Could I take your _____ now?

3. The doctor will come _____ .

4. Can I see the drink _____ ?

5. My sister works at this restaurant as a _____ .

6. I strongly _____ this book to you.

二、問答：請用英語回答下列問題。

1. 當想聽聽店家的建議時，你該怎麼說？

_____

2. 如何詢問最後點餐時間？

_____

3. 想知道這到菜辣不辣時，該如何表達？

_____

4. 想點一分熟的牛排時，該怎麼表達？

_____

5. 想付款的時候，該怎麼說？

_____

三、文法填空：請將適當的句型填入空格中。

> with / table for / in / Let us keep / glasses of
> start off with / How about / How would you like / How many

A: Hello! ① _____ are you?

B: A ② _____ 2, please.

A: Smoking or non-smoking?

B: Non-smoking, please.

B: Excuse me. Do you have a menu ③ ____ Chinese?

A: Yes. I'll bring some over to you immediately.

A: Hi. Are you ready to order now?

B: Yes. (*points to the menu*) Can I have this steak and this salad?

A: Sure. ④ _____ your steak?

B: Medium, please.

A: ⑤ _____ you, ma'am?

C: I'd like to ⑥ _____ a shrimp cocktail.

A: And for your main course?

C: Um… fish fillet, please.

A: Would you like some wine ⑦ _____ your meal?

B: Yes. 2 ⑧ _____ red wine, please.

A: OK. Can I get you anything else?

B: That's all for now. ⑨ _____ the menu for a while.

四、聽寫：請聽音檔，並將答案填入空格中。　　　　　　　　　mp3-30

A: Hello! How many are you?

B: ① _____

_____

B: Excuse me. ② _____ in Chinese?

A: Yes. I'll bring them over to you immediately.

_____

A: Hi. Are you ready to order now?

B: Yes. ③ _____

A: Sure. How would you like your steak?

B: Well done, please.

A: How about you, ma'am?

C: ④ _____

A: OK. Would you like some wine with your meal?

B: Yes. 2 glasses of red wine, please.

A: OK. Can I get you anything else?

B: ⑤ _____ Let us

keep the menu for a while. When do you take the last order?

A: 9 o'clock, sir.

第十課 練習解答‧中文翻譯

一、生詞填空：請將適當的生詞填入空格中。

1. Could you give me a clean **napkin**, please?
   能請你給我一條乾淨的餐巾嗎？

2. Could I take your **order** now?
   我可以替您點餐了嗎？

3. The doctor will come **immediately**.
   醫生馬上就會來。

4. Can I see the drink **menu**?
   我可以看飲料菜單嗎？

5. My sister works at this restaurant as a **waitress**.
   我姊姊在這家餐廳工作，當女服務員。

6. I strongly **recommend** this book to you.
   我強烈推薦這本書給你。

二、問答：請用英語回答下列問題。

1. **What do you recommend?**　　　　　　你推薦什麼？

2. **When do you take the last order?**　　最後點餐時間是幾點？

3. **Is it spicy?**　　　　　　　　　　　這個是辣的嗎？

4. **I'd like my steak rare, please.**　　　請給我一分熟的牛排。

5. **May I have the check, please?**　　　可以給我帳單嗎？

三、文法填空：請將適當的句型填入空格中。

A: Hello! ① **How many** are you?

B: A ② **table for** 2, please.

A: Smoking or non-smoking?

B: Non-smoking, please.

B: Excuse me. Do you have a menu ③ **in** Chinese?

A: Yes. I'll bring some over to you immediately.

A: Hi. Are you ready to order now?

B: Yes. (*points to the menu*) Can I have this steak and this salad?

A: Sure. ④ **How would you like** your steak?

B: Medium, please.

A: ⑤ **How about** you, ma'am?

C: I'd like to ⑥ **start off with** a shrimp cocktail.

A: And for your main course?

C: Um... fish fillet, please.

A: Would you like some wine ⑦ **with** your meal?

B: Yes. 2 ⑧ **glasses of** red wine, please.

A: OK. Can I get you anything else?

B: That's all for now. ⑨ **Let us keep** the menu for a while.

中文翻譯請見 **P. 165,167**。

四、聽寫：請聽音檔，並將答案填入空格中。

A: Hello! How many are you?

B: ① **A table for two, please.**

_____

B: Excuse me. ② **Do you have a menu** in Chinese?

A: Yes. I'll bring them over to you immediately.

_____

A: Hi. Are you ready to order now?

B: Yes. ③ **Can I have this steak?**

A: Sure. How would you like your steak?

B: Well done, please.

A: How about you, ma'am?

C: ④ **I'd like the same one, please.**

A: OK. Would you like some wine with your meal?

B: Yes. 2 glasses of red wine, please.

A: OK. Can I get you anything else?

B: ⑤ **That's all for now.** Let us keep the menu for a while. When do you take the last order?

A: 9 o'clock, sir.

A：哈囉！請問有幾位？

B：兩位。

B：不好意思，你們有中文的菜單嗎？

A：有的，我會馬上帶給您。

A：嗨，您們準備好要點餐了嗎？

B：是的。可以給我這個牛排嗎？

A：好的。您的牛排想要幾分熟呢？

B：請做全熟。

A：那，夫人您呢？

C：請給我同樣的餐點。

A：好的。您們用餐時想要配點酒嗎？

B：是的。請給我們兩杯紅酒。

A：好的。還有需要其他的嗎？

B：只要這些就好。讓我們保留一下菜單。最後點餐時間是幾點？

A：9 點，先生。

Let's Go Shopping!
一起去購物吧！

mp3-31

Dialogue A: At a Duty-Free Shop
(A: Clerk / B: Customer)

A Good afternoon! Are you looking for something specific?

B I'm just looking, thanks.

A Let me know if you need any assistance.

B Excuse me. Do you have this bag in black?

A Sure, here you are. This is the last one.

B It's beautiful. Is this on sale?

A There is a 30% discount on this.

B That's a good deal. I'll take it.

A Would that be all?

B Yes.

A That'll be 120 dollars.

B Could I get this tax-free?

A Absolutely. Could you show me your passport and fill out the form?

B Here is my passport. (*fills out the form and hands it to Clerk.*)

A Thank you. Please keep this filled tax refund form. You cannot unseal the package until you are out of the country. If you open it, you may be charged tax.

B Alright. Anything else I should know?

A Before checking-in at the airport, you'll have to take the form, the receipt, and the item you purchased to the VAT Refund Counter at the airport. Customs will examine them again.

B Got it. Thanks a lot.

Chinese Translation
中文翻譯

會話A：在免稅商店
（A：店員 / B：顧客）

A：午安！您在尋找特定的東西嗎？
B：我只是看看而已，謝謝。
A：如果您需要任何幫助，請讓我知道。

B：不好意思，這個包包有黑色的嗎？
A：當然有。這個給您。這是最後一個了。
B：真漂亮。這個有特價嗎？
A：這個有 30％的折扣。
B：那很划算。我要買下它。
A：這是所有（想買）的嗎？
B：是的。
A：總共是 120 元。
B：我可以免稅嗎？

A：當然可以。能給我看您的護照並填寫這個表格嗎？

B：這是我的護照。（填寫表格並交給店員）

A：謝謝您。這份填好的退稅表請您留著。直到離境前都不能拆開包裝，如果您打開了，就可能會被課稅。

B：沒問題。還有其他我該知道的嗎？

A：在機場辦理登機之前，您必須帶著這個表格、收據及您買的物品，到機場內的增值稅退款櫃檯。海關會再次查驗。

B：我了解了。非常謝謝。

Vocabulary 生詞

mp3-32

❶ specific (adj.) 特定的

❷ assistance (n.) 協助

❸ absolutely (adv.) 絕對地

❹ unseal (v.) 開封

❺ package (n.) 包裝

❻ tax (n.) 稅

tax-free (adj.) 免稅的

❼ refund (n. / v.) 退款

❽ counter (n.) 櫃檯

purchase (v.) 購買

examine (v.) 查驗

VAT = value-added tax 增值稅（是一種消費稅）

1

當店員對你說「Can I help you?」（我可以幫你嗎？），你可以回答：

1 I'm just looking, thank you.	我只是在看看，謝謝。
2 I'm looking for ...	我在找……
3 Yes, please.	是的，請（幫我）。
4 Would you show me that?	可以給我看那個嗎？
5 Do you have any recommendations for souvenir for my friends?	有任何推薦送給我朋友的紀念品嗎？

2

對商品有疑問時，你可以說：

1 Can I pick it up?	我可以拿起來看嗎？
2 What is this made of?	這是什麼做的？
3 Can you do a price check for me?	能幫我查價格嗎？
4 Does it have a warranty?	這個有保固嗎？
5 When is the expiration date?	到期日是何時？

3

如何議價？

1 Won't you give me a little discount?	不給我一點折扣嗎？
2 Can I get this tax-free?	我可以用免稅買這個嗎？
3 Could you give me a discount if I buy 3?	如果我買 3 件，能給我折扣嗎？
4 Do you have anything less expensive?	有便宜一點的東西嗎？

4 如何表達購買意願？

1 **I will take this.** 我要買下這個。

2 **I would like 5 of these.** 我想要 5 個這個。

3 **Let me think about it.** 讓我考慮一下。

4 **Can I look around a little more?** 我可以再逛一下嗎？

5 想指定包裝方式時，你可以說：

1 **Could you wrap them separately, please?** 能請你分別包裝它們嗎？

2 **Can I get this gift-wrapped?** 可以幫我把這個包裝成禮物嗎？

3 **Can I have 3 small bags, please?** 請問我可以有 3 個小袋子嗎？

6 需要退貨或更換商品時，你可以說：

1 **I'd like to return this.** 我想要退回這個。

2 **Could I exchange this for a different one?** 我可以用其他的更換這個嗎？

3 **I would like a refund / an exchange, please.** 我想要退費／更換商品。

Grammar 文法

01 be looking for 名詞 找尋某件物品

例 I am looking for some Australian made toys.　　我正在找些澳洲製造的玩具。

Are you looking for anything in particular? 你正在找任何特定的東西嗎？

02 Let me know if... 如果……，請讓我知道。

例 Let me know if you have any problems.　　如果你有任何問題，請讓我知道。

Please let me know if there are any changes.　　如果有任何更動，請讓我知道。

03 用「one」（一個）替代可數名詞

例 A: Did you bring an umbrella?　　你有帶雨傘嗎？

B: Yes. I've got one.　　有，我帶了一把（雨傘）。

My computer is broken. I have to buy a new one.　　我的電腦壞了。我必須買一台新的（電腦）。

04 Anything else ...? (=Is there anything else ...?) 還有其他……的嗎？

例 Anything else I should know?　　還有其他是我該知道的嗎？

Anything else you like?　　還有其他是你喜歡的嗎？

05 before 動詞 ing 型（動名詞） 做某件事之前

例 I read a book before going to bed.　　我睡前看書。

We bought some presents before coming here.　　我們來這裡之前買了些禮物。

06 用「形容詞子句」修飾前方的名詞

例 This is a picture I took in Taipei. 這張照片是我在台北拍的。

The book I read yesterday was interesting. 我昨天讀的這本書很有趣。

一、生詞填空：請將適當的生詞填入空格中。

> refund / counter / specific / package / examined
> purchase / absolutely / assistance

1. A _____ reached me this afternoon.

2. Do you need any _____ ?

3. I will _____ the money to you.

4. The police _____ the footage.

5. I think that cake will _____ sell.

6. The admission ticket _____ is over there.

7. He could not explain the _____ content at a meeting.

8. If you _____ more than 100 dollars of the target item, you will receive a 10-dollar gift certificate.

二、問答：請用英語回答下列問題。

1. 想請店員推薦買給朋友的禮物時，該如何詢問？

_____

2. 想詢問商品是否附有保固時，該怎麼說？

_____

3. 如何詢問是否能免稅？

_____

4. 想知道是否有便宜一點的商品時，該怎麼問？

_____

三、文法填空：請將適當的句型填入空格中。

> Anything else / fill out / out of / Let me know
> just looking / Before / in / looking for

A: Good afternoon! Are you ① _____ something specific?

B: I'm ② _____ , thanks.

A: ③ _____ if you need any assistance.

___

B: Excuse me. Do you have this bag ④ _____ black?

A: Sure, here you are.

B: It's beautiful! I'll take it.

A: OK! That'll be 120 dollars.

B: Could I get this tax-free?

A: Absolutely. Could you show me your passport and ⑤ _____ the form?

B: Here is my passport. (*fills out the form and hands it to A*)

A: Thank you. Please keep this filled tax refund form. You cannot unseal the package until you are ⑥ _____ the country.

B: Alright. ⑦ _____ I should know?

A: ⑧ _____ checking-in at the airport, you'll have to take the form, the receipt, and the item you purchased to the VAT Refund Counter at the airport.

B: Got it. Thanks a lot.

四、聽寫：請聽音檔，並將答案填入空格中。 mp3-33

A: Good morning! May I help you?

B: Yes. ① _____

A: Let me check... Here you are. This is the last one.

B: It's beautiful! ② _____

A: Of course.

B: ③ _____

A: There is a 30% discount on this.

B: ④ _____

⑤ _____

A: Would that be all?

B: Yes.

A: That'll be 120 dollars.

B: ⑥ _____

A: Absolutely. Could you show me your passport?

B: Here is my passport.

第十一課 練習解答 · 中文翻譯

一、生詞填空：請將適當的生詞填入空格中。

1. A **package** reached me this afternoon.
   今天下午有個包裹送達給我。

2. Do you need any **assistance**?
   你需要任何協助嗎？

3. I will **refund** the money to you.
   我會退還錢給你。

4. The police **examined** the footage.
   警察查驗影片。

5. I think that cake will **absolutely** sell.
   我認為那個蛋糕絕對會大賣的。

6. The admission ticket **counter** is over there.
   入場券櫃檯在那邊。

7. He could not explain the **specific** content at a meeting.
   他無法在會議上解釋具體內容。

8. If you **purchase** more than 100 dollars of the target item, you will receive a 10-dollar gift certificate.
   如果購買超過 100 美元的目標商品，您將獲得 10 美元的禮券。

二、問答：請用英語回答下列問題。

1. **Do you have any recommendations for souvenir for my friends?**　有任何推薦送給我朋友的紀念品嗎？

2. **Does it have a warranty?**　這個有保固嗎？

3. **Can I get this tax-free?**　我可以用免稅買這個嗎？

4. **Do you have anything less expensive?**　有便宜一點的東西嗎？

三、文法填空：請將適當的句型填入空格中。

A: Good afternoon! Are you ① looking for something specific?

B: I'm ② just looking, thanks.

A: ③ Let me know if you need any assistance.

B: Excuse me. Do you have this bag ④ in black?

A: Sure, here you are.

B: It's beautiful! I'll take it.

A: OK! That'll be 120 dollars.

B: Could I get this tax-free?

A: Absolutely. Could you show me your passport and ⑤ fill out the form?

B: Here is my passport. (*fills out the form and hands it to A*)

A: Thank you. Please keep this filled tax refund form. You cannot unseal the package until you are ⑥ out of the country.

B: Alright. ⑦ Anything else I should know?

A: ⑧ Before checking in at the airport, you'll have to take the form, the receipt, and the item you purchased to the VAT Refund Counter at the airport.

B: Got it. Thanks a lot.

中文翻譯請見 P. 184-185。

四、聽寫：請聽音檔，並將答案填入空格中。

A: Good morning! May I help you?

B: Yes. ① Do you have any jackets in black?

A: Let me check... Here you are. This is the last one.

B: It's beautiful! ② **Can I pick it up?**

A: Of course.

B: ③ **Is this on sale?**

A: There is a 30% discount on this.

B: ④ **That's a good deal.** ⑤ **I will take it.**

A: Would that be all?

B: Yes.

A: That'll be 120 dollars.

B: ⑥ **Could I get this tax-free?**

A: Absolutely. Could you show me your passport?

B: Here is my passport.

中文翻譯

A：早安！我可以幫您嗎？

B：是的。你有任何黑色的夾克嗎？

A：讓我找一下……在這裡。這是最後一件了。

B：很漂亮！我可以拿起來看看嗎？

A：當然可以。

B：這有特價嗎？

A：這個有 30% 的折扣。

B：很划算。我要買下它。

A：這是所有（想買）的嗎？

B：是的。

A：總共是 120 元。

B：我可以免稅嗎？

A：絕對可以的。能給我看您的護照？

B：這是我的護照。

My Bag Was Stolen!

我的包包被偷了！

Dialogue A: At the Police Station

(A: Tourist / B: Policeman)

A Excuse me, my bag was stolen!

B Where was your bag stolen?

A I was in the accessory shop and looking at some necklaces. Then, someone suddenly pulled my bag. It happened all too fast for me to pull it back.

B Okay, I will help you file a police report for stolen property. What kind of bag was it?

A It's a small blue handbag.

B What was in the bag?

A All of my valuables were in there.

B Please tell me every stolen item.

A My passport, wallet, mobile phone, and some cosmetics.

B How much money was in your wallet?

A About 300 dollars in cash and 2 credit cards.

B I think you should call the credit card company, and suspend your credit cards as soon as possible.

A Oh yes, you're right! I've got to call them.

B Here is the completed police report. Next, you'll need to go to your country's embassy to report a lost passport.

A Okay. Thank you very much.

Chinese Translation
中文翻譯

會話A：在警察局
（A：旅客 / B：警察）

A：抱歉，我的包包被偷了！

B：你的包包是在哪裡被偷的？

A：我在飾品店裡，正看著一些項鍊。然後，有人突然拉了我的包包。但一切發生得太快了，我來不及把包包拉回來。

B：好的。我會協助你填寫失竊報案證明。是什麼樣的包包呢？

A：它是個小的藍色手提包。

B：手提包裡有什麼？

A：我所有的貴重物品都在裡面。

B：請告訴我每一個被偷的物品。

A：我的護照、錢包、手機和一些化妝品。

B：你的錢包裡有多少錢？

A：大約 300 美元的現金和 2 張信用卡。

B：我認為你應該致電信用卡公司，並盡快暫停你的信用卡。

A：喔，你說的對！我必須打電話給他們。
B：這是填寫完的報案證明。接下來，你需要去你國家的大使館通報遺失護照。
A：好的，非常謝謝你。

Vocabulary 生詞

1 stolen (adj.) （steal 的過去分詞）偷；盜竊

2 accessory (n.) 飾品

3 necklace (n.) 項鍊

4 suddenly (adv.) 突然地

5 pull (v.) 拉

6 fast (adv. / adj.) 快速地

7 theft (n.) 偷竊

8 handbag (n.) 手提包

9 **valuable (adj. / n.)** 貴重的；值錢的（物品）

10 **wallet (n.)** 錢包

11 **cosmetic (n.)** 化妝品

12 **possible (adj.)** 可能

13 **embassy (n.)** 大使館；領事館

1

遇到竊盜等狀況，需要請求幫忙時，你可以說：

1 Please call the police.	請打電話給警察。
2 Stop! Thief!	不要跑！小偷！
3 Somebody, catch him!	誰快來抓住他！
4 Where is the nearest police station?	最近的警察局在哪裡？

2

當你失去私人物品時，你可以說：

1 I've lost my camera.	我遺失了我的相機。
2 I left my bag on the taxi.	我把我的包包留在計程車上了。
3 Have you seen a bag that was sitting here?	你有在這裡看到一個包包嗎？
4 Where is the lost and found office?	失物招領處在哪裡？
5 My iPhone was stolen.	我的 iPhone 被偷了。
6 My wallet was pickpocketed on the train.	我的錢包在電車上被扒走了。

3

需要詳細說明被偷的東西時，你可以說：

1 It's a big black shoulder bag with my wallet, passport and camera in it.	它是一個大的黑色肩包，裡面有我的錢包、護照和相機。
2 I had no cash in my wallet but some credit cards.	我的錢包裡除了信用卡之外，沒有現金。

4 遭遇竊盜後，欲採取後續行動，你可以說：

1 **I want to file a police report for stolen property.**　　我要為失竊物品做報案。

2 **Would you tell me the phone number of the Taipei Economic and Cultural Representative office?**　　您能告訴我台北經濟文化代表處的電話號碼嗎？

3 **Please suspend my credit card immediately.**　　請馬上暫停我的信用卡。

4 **Please stop my cell phone service.**　　請停止我的手機（服務）。

5 **Where can I get my passport reissued?**　　在哪裡可以重新簽發護照？

6 **What documents do I need to provide in order to request a reissue?**　　我需要提供什麼文件才能請求重新簽發？

01 **be + 動詞過去分詞** 被⋯⋯（被動語態）

例 This bag is made in Italy. 　　　　　　　這個包是在義大利被製造的。

Is English used in your country? 　　　　您所在的國家使用英語嗎？（英語在您的國家被使用嗎？）

02 **too ... to ...** 太⋯⋯而不能⋯⋯

例 The suitcase is too heavy to carry. 　　　行李箱太重了，無法隨身攜帶。

I was too tired to go to dinner with my 我太累了，無法和朋友一起去吃晚餐。
friends.

03 **英語中的形容詞語序（Adjective order）**

形容詞種類與排序	例
1 Opinion 主觀意見	pretty, delicious, difficult...
2 Size 尺寸	big, little, tall...
3 Age 年紀	old, young, ancient...
4 Shape 形狀	round, flat, square...
5 Color 顏色	black, red, dark...
6 Origin 出身	Japanese, Asian, Oriental...
7 Material 材料	cotton, leather, wooden...
8 Purpose 目的	shopping, coffee-drinking, knitting...

例

冠詞	數量	形容詞								名詞
		Opinion	Size	Age	Shape	Color	Origin	Material	Purpose	
	2		tall	young			Japanese			men
	3					red		leather		bags
a		pretty				pink				rose

04 **I think you should 動詞原形** 我覺得你應該……

例 I think you should go by taxi. 我覺得你應該搭計程車過去。

I think you shouldn't spend a lot of money in casinos. 我覺得你不應該在賭場裡花這麼多錢。

05 **as soon as possible** 盡快地

例 I will go home as soon as possible. 我會盡快回家。

Please give me an answer as soon as possible. 請盡快給我答案。

Exercise
練習

一、生詞填空：請將適當的生詞填入空格中。

| wallet / possible / valuable / theft / fast |
| accessories / pulled / suddenly |

1. He _____ the rope with all his strength.

2. It _____ started to rain.

3. These kinds of stamps are _____.

4. Please reply as soon as _____.

5. I can run very _____.

6. All of these _____ are handmade.

7. The thief stole all the money out of the old man's _____.

8. I would like to report a _____.

二、問答：請用英語回答下列問題。

1. 當你將 iPhone 遺留在計程車上時，該怎麼說？

_____

2. 當想描述那是一個長長的黑色皮革錢包時，該怎麼說？

_____

3. 想請警察提供一份失竊報案證明時，該怎麼說？

_____

4. 當想立即停止使用信用卡時，該怎麼說？

_____

三、文法填空：請將適當的句型填入空格中。

> too fast / every / I've got to / Where was / All of
> What kind of / as soon as possible / How much

A: Excuse me, my bag was stolen.

B: ① _____ your bag stolen?

A: I was in the accessory shop and looking at some necklaces. Then, someone suddenly

pulled my bag. It happened all ② _____ for me to pull it back.

B: Okay, I will help you file a police report for stolen property.

③ _____ bag was it?

A: It's a small blue handbag.

B: What was in the bag?

A: ④ _____ my valuables are in there.

B: Please tell me ⑤ _____ stolen item.

A: My passport, wallet, mobile phone, and some cosmetics.

B: ⑥ _____ money was in your wallet?

A: About 300 dollars in cash and 2 credit cards.

B: I think you should call the credit card company, and suspend your credit cards

⑦ _____ .

A: Oh, yes, you're right! ⑧ _____ call them.

B: Here is the completed police report. Next, you'll need to go to your country's

embassy to report a lost passport.

A: Okay. Thank you very much.

A: ① _____

B: Where was your wallet stolen?

A: I was in the accessory shop and looking at some necklaces.

　　Then, ② _____

B: What kind of wallet was it?

A: ③ _____

B: Please tell me every stolen item in the wallet

A: There were ④ _____

B: How much money was in your wallet?

A: ⑤ _____ were in there, too.

B: I think you should contact your credit card companies, and suspend your credit cards

　　as soon as possible.

A: Oh, yes, that's right! ⑥ _____

第十二課 練習解答・中文翻譯

一、生詞填空：請將適當的生詞填入空格中。

1. He **pulled** the rope with all his strength.
   他盡全力拉那根繩子。

2. It **suddenly** started to rain.
   突然開始下雨。

3. These kinds of stamps are **valuable**.
   這樣的郵票很珍貴。

4. Please reply as soon as **possible**.
   請盡可能快速答覆我。

5. I can run very **fast**.
   我可以跑得非常快。

6. All of these **accessories** are handmade.
   這些所有的飾品配件都是手工製作的。

7. The thief stole all the money out of the old man's **wallet**.
   小偷把老人錢包裡所有的錢都偷走了。

8. I would like to report a **theft**.
   我想為一樁盜竊報案。

二、問答：請用英語回答下列問題。

1. **I left my iPhone on the taxi.**　　　我把 iPhone 留在計程車上了。

2. **It's a long black leather wallet.**　　　它是一個長的黑色皮革錢包。

3. **Could you provide me with a completed police report?**　　　能請您給我一份填寫完的失竊報案證明嗎？

4. **Please suspend my credit card immediately.**　　　請立即暫停我的信用卡。

三、文法填空：請將適當的句型填入空格中。

A: Excuse me, my bag was stolen.

B: ① **Where was** your bag stolen?

A: I was in the accessory shop and looking at some necklaces. Then, someone suddenly pulled my bag. It happened all ② **too fast** for me to pull it back.

B: Okay, I will help you file a police report for stolen property. ③ **What kind of** bag was it?

A: It's a small blue handbag.

B: What was in the bag?

A: ④ **All of** my valuables were in there.

B: Please tell me ⑤ **every** stolen item.

A: My passport, wallet, mobile phone, and some cosmetics.

B: ⑥ **How much** money was in your wallet?

A: About 300 dollars in cash and 2 credit cards.

B: I think you should call the credit card company, and suspend your credit cards ⑦ **as soon as possible**.

A: Oh, yes, you're right! ⑧ **I've got to** call them.

B: Here is the completed police report. Next, you'll need to go to your country's embassy to report a lost passport.

A: Okay. Thank you very much.

中文翻譯請見 **P. 200-201**。

四、聽寫：請聽音檔，並將答案填入空格中。

A: ① **Excuse me, I lost my wallet.**

B: Where was your wallet stolen?

A: I was in the accessory shop and looking at some necklaces. Then, ② **someone suddenly pulled my bag.**

B: What kind of wallet was it?

A: ③ **It was a small blue one.**

B: Please tell me every stolen item in the wallet.

A: There were ④ **my passport, some money and a city map.**

B: How much money was in your wallet?

A: ⑤ **Only 30 dollars in cash, but 3 credit cards** were in there, too.

B: I think you should contact your credit card companies, and suspend your credit cards as soon as possible.

A: Oh, yes, that's right! ⑥ **I've got to call them.**

中文翻譯

A：抱歉，我遺失了我的錢包。

B：你的錢包是在哪裡被偷的？

A：我在飾品店裡，正看著一些項鍊。然後，有人突然拉了我的包包。

B：它是什麼樣的錢包？

A：它是個藍色的小錢包。

B：請告訴我錢包裡每一個被偷的物品。

A：裡面有我的護照、一些錢和一份城市地圖。

B：你的錢包裡有多少錢？

A：只有 30 元現金，但還有 3 張信用卡在裡面。

B：我認為你應該聯絡信用卡公司，並盡快暫停你的信用卡。

A：對，沒錯！我必須打電話給他們。

Getting Medical Treatment While Traveling 旅途中就醫

mp3-37

Dialogue A: At the Clinic Reception
(A: Receptionist / B: Patient)

A Hi. Do you have an appointment?

B No, I don't, but I need to see a doctor.

A Ok. Please fill out this form. Do you have an insurance card with you?

B No, I don't have one. I will pay the full treatment cost, but can I have a medical certificate for my insurance claim back in Taiwan?

A No problem.

Chinese Translation
中文翻譯

會話A：在診所櫃檯
（A：櫃檯人員 / B：病人）

A：嗨，您有預約嗎？

B：不，我沒有，但我需要看醫生。

A：好，請填寫這張表格。您是否有隨身攜帶保險卡？

B：不，我沒有保險卡。我會支付全額治療費用，但可以幫我開一份就醫證明嗎？以便回到台灣後申請保險理賠。

A：沒問題。

Dialogue B: Getting a Diagnosis
(B: Patient / C: Doctor)

C What's going on?

B I am not feeling well. I've got a headache and a running nose.

C How long have you had these symptoms?

B Since last Saturday, so around 3 days.

C I see. Let me check your temperature. It's 38.5 degrees Celsius. Do you have any other symptoms?

B I've also been coughing a lot.

C Ok. You've probably got the flu. Do you have any allergies?

B Yes, I am allergic to eggs.

C Are you taking any medicine?

B Yes, I've been taking pain-killers since I started feeling sick.

C Are you pregnant?

B No, I'm not.

C Ok. I will write you a prescription.

B Thank you.

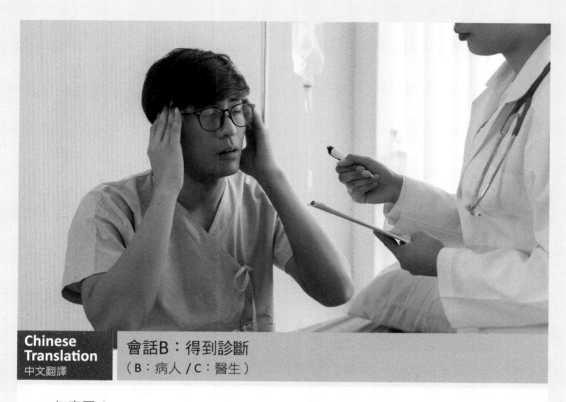

Chinese Translation
中文翻譯

會話B：得到診斷
（B：病人 / C：醫生）

C：怎麼了？
B：我感覺不舒服。一直頭痛和流鼻涕。
C：你有這些症狀多久了？
B：自從上週六起，所以是 3 天左右。
C：我明白了。讓我檢查你的體溫。是攝氏 38.5 度。你還有其他症狀嗎？
B：我也一直不斷咳嗽。
C：好，你應該是得到流感了。你有任何過敏嗎？
B：有，我對雞蛋過敏。
C：你正在服用任何藥物嗎？
B：是的，自從我開始感覺生病以來，我一直在服用止痛藥。
C：你有懷孕嗎？
B：不，我沒有。
C：好，我會開處方給你。
B：謝謝。

1 appointment (n.) 預約

2 insurance (n.) 保險

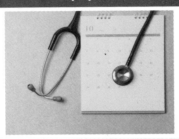

3 treatment (n.) 治療

4 symptom (n.) 症狀

5 temperature (n.) 溫度，體溫

6 Celsius (n.) 攝氏

7 probably (adv.) 可能；或許

8 allergy (n.) 過敏

9 **pain-killer (n.)** 止痛藥

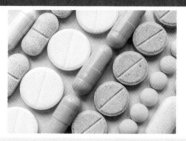

10 **pregnant (adj.)** 懷孕

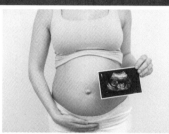

11 **prescription (n.)** 處方

12 **diagnosis (n.)** 診斷；診療

My Body Parts 我的身體部位

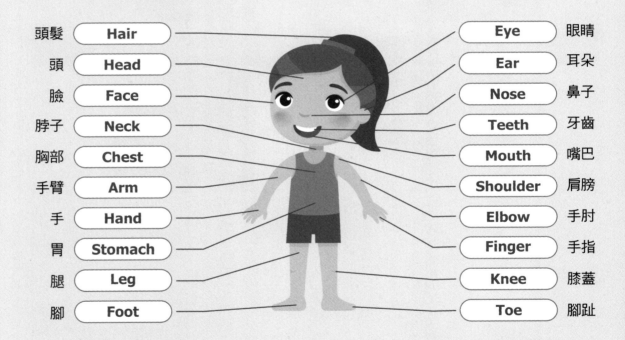

頭髮 (Hair)

頭 (Head)

臉 (Face)

脖子 (Neck)

胸部 (Chest)

手臂 (Arm)

手 (Hand)

胃 (Stomach)

腿 (Leg)

腳 (Foot)

(Eye) 眼睛

(Ear) 耳朵

(Nose) 鼻子

(Teeth) 牙齒

(Mouth) 嘴巴

(Shoulder) 肩膀

(Elbow) 手肘

(Finger) 手指

(Knee) 膝蓋

(Toe) 腳趾

1 需要描述自己的症狀時，你可以說：

1 **I feel**   **sick** 不舒服

                dizzy 頭昏

                cold 冷

                dull 沒有精神

                nauseous 噁心；想嘔吐的

                sick to my stomach 反胃；想吐

2 **I have**   **diarrhea** 腹瀉

                a cold 感冒

                a (high) fever 發（高）燒

                a running / stuffy nose 鼻水／鼻塞

                a headache / toothache / stomachache / backache

                頭痛／牙痛／胃痛／背痛

                a sore throat 喉嚨痛

                a cough 咳嗽

                high / low blood pressure 高／低血壓

3 **I am**   **pregnant** 懷孕

                allergic to ... 對……過敏

                constipated 便祕

4 **I**   **injured my leg.** 傷了我的腿。

                broke my finger. 弄斷了我的手指。

2 與藥物相關的短句有：

1 **Are there any side effects?** 　　　有任何副作用嗎？

2 **When should I take this tablet and** 　我應該何時服用多少顆藥片？
how many?

3 **Do you have any pain-killers?** 　　你有止痛藥嗎？

4 **Please take this medicine with meals.** 請隨餐服用這種藥。

5 **Please take 2 tablets once every 4** 　請每 4 小時服用 2 顆藥片。
hours.

6 **Where is the nearest drugstore?** 　最近的藥局在哪裡？

3 診斷時常見的問答有：

	問題	回答
1	What are your symptoms? 你的症狀是什麼？	I have a sore throat. 我喉嚨痛。
2	When did your symptom start? 你的症狀是何時開始的？	Last night. 昨晚。
3	Are you allergic to anything or any medication? 你對什麼東西或什麼藥物過敏嗎？	Yes, I'm allergic to eggs. 有，我對雞蛋過敏。 Yes, I'm allergic to aspirin. 有，我對阿斯匹林過敏。 No, I'm not allergic to anything. 不，我沒有對任何東西過敏。

4	Do you have any appetite? 你有任何胃口嗎？	Yes, I do. 是的，我有。 No, I'm not. 不，我沒有。
5	Are you pregnant? 你有懷孕嗎？	Yes, I'm 4 months pregnant. 是的，我懷孕 4 個月了。 No, I'm not. 不，我沒有。
6	Are you taking any medicine regularly? 你有定期吃任何藥嗎？	Yes, I'm taking medicine for high blood pressure. 是的，我吃高血壓的藥。 No, I'm not. 不，我沒有。
7	What is your blood type? 你的血型是什麼？	A / B / O / AB

4

關於治療和檢查的短句有：

1 **You need to be hospitalized.** 　你需要住院。

2 **Let me take an X-ray of your chest.** 　讓我對你的胸部進行 X 光檢查。

3 **You need an operation.** 　你需要動手術。

4 **I will give you a shot (an injection).** 　我給你打一針（注射）。

5 **I will check your blood pressure.** 　我會量你的血壓。

Grammar 文法

01 **Do you have 名詞 with you?** 你現在身上有某件物品嗎？

例 Do you have money with you?   你身上有錢嗎？

Do you have a mobile phone with you now?   你現在身上有帶手機嗎？

02 **back in 場所** 回到某場所

例 He is back in Taiwan now.   他現在回到台灣了。

I can only relax when I'm back in my hometown.   我只有在回到家鄉時才能放鬆。

03 **since 時間點** ～自……以來，從……至今

例 I have been feeling bad since last weekend.   自上週末以來，我一直感到很內疚。

We have known each other since childhood.   我們從孩童時期就互相認識。

04 **How long have you 過去分詞？** 你……多久了？

例 How long have you been in Taiwan?   你來台灣多久了？

How long have you known him?   你已經認識他多久了？

05 **(I) have got... = have** 有

例 I've got a driver's license.   我有駕照。

We're terribly sorry, but we haven't got any change.   我們非常抱歉，但我們沒有任何零錢。

一、生詞填空：請將適當的生詞填入空格中。

| pregnant / treatment / allergy / insurance |
| Celsius / symptoms / appointment / diagnosis |

1. The doctor made an incorrect _____ .

2. What time is your dentist's _____ ?

3. Though you are a famous actor, we cannot give you any special _____ .

4. I'm 6 months _____ .

5. I recommend that you have a car _____ .

6. Ice melts at zero degrees _____ .

7. I have an _____ to seafood.

8. How long does it take for _____ to appear?

二、問答：請用英語回答下列問題。

1. 當解釋有腹瀉時，該怎麼說？

_____

2. 如何請問對方是否有止痛藥？

_____

3. 當你對堅果過敏時，該怎麼說？

_____

4. 當想表達胃口不好時，該怎麼說？

_____

三、文法填空：請將適當的句型填入空格中。

> How long have you / I've got / with you / Since
> back in / Let me check / How / I have been / What are

A: ① _____ may I help you? Do you have an appointment?

B: No, I don't, but I need to see a doctor.

A: Ok. Please fill out this form. Do you have an insurance card ② _____ ?

B: No, I don't have one. I will pay the full treatment cost, but can I have a medical

certificate for my insurance claim ③ _____ Taiwan?

A: No problem.

(*patient enters the doctor's office*)

C: ④ _____ your symptoms?

B: ⑤ _____ a headache and a running nose.

C: ⑥ _____ had these symptoms?

B: ⑦ _____ last Saturday, so around 3 days.

C: I see. ⑧ _____ your temperature. It's 38.5 degrees Celsius. Do

you have any other symptoms?

B: I've also been coughing a lot.

C: You probably got the flu. Do you have any allergies?

B: Yes, I am allergic to eggs.

C: Are you taking any medicine?

B: ⑨ _____ taking pain-killers since I started feeling sick.

C: Are you pregnant?

B: No, I am not.

C: I will write you a prescription.

B: OK, thank you.

四、聽寫：請聽音檔，並將答案填入空格中。 mp3-39

A: How may I help you? Do you have an appointment?

B: ① _____

A: Can I have your name?

B: Yi-Ling Chen.

A: Ms. Chen, do you have an insurance card with you?

B: No, I don't have one. ② _____,

   but can I have a medical certificate for my insurance claim?

A: No problem.

(*patient enters the doctor's office*)

C: What's going on?

B: ③ _____

C: How long have you had this symptom?

B: ④ _____

C: I see. Do you have any other symptoms?

B: ⑤ _____

C: Ok, I will write you a prescription. Do you have any allergies?

B: ⑥ _____

C: Are you taking any medicine?

B: ⑦ _____

C: Please avoid eating spicy and greasy food for a while.

B: OK, thank you.

第十三課 練習解答・中文翻譯

一、生詞填空：請將適當的生詞填入空格中。

1. The doctor made an incorrect **diagnosis**.
   醫生做了不正確的診斷。

2. What time is your dentist's **appointment**?
   什麼時候是你的牙醫預約？

3. Though you are a famous actor, we cannot give you any special **treatment**.
   儘管你是著名演員，但我們不能給您特殊的待遇。

4. I'm 6 months **pregnant**.
   我懷孕六個月了。

5. I recommend that you have a car **insurance**.
   我建議你買個汽車保險。

6. Ice melts at zero degrees **Celsius**.
   冰融化在攝氏零度時。

7. I have an **allergy** to seafood.
   我對海鮮有過敏。

8. How long does it take for **symptoms** to appear?
   症狀出現需要多長時間？

二、問答：請用英語回答下列問題。

1. **I have diarrhea.**   我腹瀉了。

2. **Do you have any pain-killers?**   你有止痛藥嗎？

3. **I am allergic to nuts.**   我對堅果過敏。

4. **I do not have any appetite.**   我沒有任何胃口。

三、文法填空：請將適當的句型填入空格中。

A: ① **How** may I help you? Do you have an appointment?

B: No, I don't, but I need to see a doctor.

A: Ok. Please fill out this form. Do you have an insurance card ② **with you**?

B: No, I don't have one. I will pay the full treatment cost, but can I have a medical certificate for my insurance claim ③ **back in** Taiwan?

A: No problem.

(*patient enters the doctor's office*)

C: ④ **What are** your symptoms?

B: ⑤ **I've got** a headache and a running nose.

C: ⑥ **How long have you** had these symptoms?

B: ⑦ **Since** last Saturday, so around 3 days.

C: I see. ⑧ **Let me check** your temperature. It's 38.5 degrees Celsius. Do you have any other symptoms?

B: I've also been coughing a lot.

C: You probably got the flu. Do you have any allergies?

B: Yes, I am allergic to eggs.

C: Are you taking any medicine?

B: ⑨ **I have been** taking pain-killers since I started feeling sick.

C: Are you pregnant?

B: No, I am not.

C: I will write you a prescription.

B: OK, thank you.

中文翻譯請見 P. 215,217。

四、聽寫：請聽音檔，並將答案填入空格中。

A: How may I help you? Do you have an appointment?

B: ① **Yes, I have an appointment.**

A: Can I have your name?

B: Yi-Ling Chen.

A: Ms. Chen, do you have an insurance card with you?

B: No, I don't have one. ② **I will pay the full treatment cost,** but can I have a medical certificate for my insurance claim?

A: No problem.

(*patient enters the doctor's office*)

C: What's going on?

B: ③ **I have a stomachache.**

C: How long have you had this symptom?

B: ④ **For 2 days.**

C: I see. Do you have any other symptoms?

B: ⑤ **I also have diarrhea and I am vomiting.**

C: OK, I will write you a prescription. Do you have any allergies?

B: ⑥ **Yes, I'm allergic to milk.**

C: Are you taking any medicine?

B: ⑦ **No, I am not.**

C: Please avoid eating spicy and greasy food for a while.

B: OK, thank you.